THE MANIACS AND THE RAT BANQUET

On Tuesday, November 1, 1983, the international right-wing terrorist organization known as SADIF—the Sons and Daughters in Freedom—invaded forty-nine madhouses in Canada, Mexico, and the United States, and released 615 maniacs into the world.

On the same day in New York City, at the famous Waldorf-Astoria Hotel, backers of the newly founded Federalist-Liberal party sponsored a gala fund-raising event. The festivities featured main dishes of rat stroganoff, roasted rat, and rat parmesan. The FLP also announced its very strong presence in next year's elections. The public eating of rodents tied in nicely with the FLP's electioneering slogan: THROW THE RATS OUT!

And at the CIA, the one they called the Old Man knew the two events that day were no coincidence.

Also in **THE ASSASSIN** *series from Pinnacle Books*

THE ASSASSIN

#4 DEATH'S RUNNING MATE
JOHN D. REVERE

PINNACLE BOOKS   NEW YORK

THE ASSASSIN #4: DEATH'S RUNNING MATE

An original Pinnacle Books edition, published for the first time
anywhere.

First printing/January 1985

ISBN: 0-523-42167-2

Can. ISBN: 0-523-43156-2

Printed in the United States of America

PINNACLE BOOKS, INC.
1430 Broadway
New York, New York 10018

9 8 7 6 5 4 3 2 1

for John Phelps,
with gratitude

DEATH'S RUNNING MATE

ONE

"You're going to destroy the whole town, Justin?"

Justin Perry regarded Bob Dante with a cool, steady gaze. "I'm going to destroy it, Dante."

"My God!" Dante turned very pale. "There must be *ten or fifteen thousand people* in that town!"

Justin nodded. "There are 12,175 men and women, to be exact. But no children. Not one individual under twenty years of age. And no children at all."

Now, Dante frowned. "A town without children? It sounds impossible. I guess it means that nobody's fucking."

"I wish it were that simple," Justin said. "People *are* fucking. It means something else, something far more ominous and diabolical. And that's why it has to be destroyed."

Dante seemed unusually excited; and that surprised Justin. Dante knew all about the town—why did he suppose all that TNT had been planted?—and he knew what had to be done, and why it had to be done. Still, he protested, as though pleading for a lover's life.

"Isn't there some other way, Justin? You can't really be serious!"

1

"I'm very serious," Justin Perry said. And he was. Planning to kill that many people made him feel somewhat like God.

On Tuesday, November 1, 1983, the international right-wing terrorist organization known as SADIF—the Sons and Daughters in Freedom—invaded forty-nine madhouses in Canada, Mexico, and the United States, and released 615 maniacs into the world.

On the same day in New York City at the famous Waldorf-Astoria Hotel, backers of the newly founded Federalist-Liberal party (FLP)—a colorful coalition of dissident Democrats and Republicans, homosexuals, blacks, Hispanics, Jews, cripples, females, and the like—sponsored a gala fund-raising event at which the main dishes were rat strogonoff, roasted rat, and rat parmesan. The Federalist-Liberal party also announced its very strong presence in next year's national elections.

The public eating of rodents tied in nicely with the FLP's electioneering slogan: THROW THE RATS OUT; although some attendees at the affair were later photographed throwing the rats up. The photographs—several of which made *People* magazine—soon became famous, and rat meat became such a popular food, especially among the wealthy, that certain butchers asked for, and received, permission to sell the rodent meat on a nationwide scale.

Experts on such matters said that rat meat was high in protein and trytophan amino acid, which is vital to the body's functions. They also said that rat meat contained "testosterone hormone, a chemical substance which can stimulate the libido in cases of sexual dysfunction." To support the latter claim, nutritionists pointed to the fast reproduction of rats, and to the fact that there are far more rats than peope in the world; and sales of the product soared among persons needing a lift to limp genitals.

Exactly one year after the notorious New York banquet, the Federalist-Liberal party had made more than good in its word about being a presence in the forthcoming elections for president of the United States. Its charismatic candidate—a beautiful, thirty-seven-year-old woman named Andrea McKay, who was said to thrive on champagne and rat meat—had steamrolled over all other contending candidates, and was set to confront John Jay Hilton, the incumbent Republican president, in tomorrow's national elections. It would be the first time in American history that a third-party candidate, and a woman at that, would have the chance to slug it out with a sitting president. All polls predicted that Andrea McKay would win over Hilton by a very comfortable margin.

On election night, in the unseasonable warmth of a midwestern plain, sheriffs' deputies, newspaper reporters, and government agents with hysterical hounds on leashes, slammed through the night following the trail of a naked white woman who had thus far eluded them. While this strange hunt was going on, Justin Perry and Bob Dante, of the U.S. Central Intelligence Agency, had made their comments about the need to destroy the town without children and were now giving their muscular bodies up to the tender mercies of two chesty women at a massage parlor in the seamier section of the nation's capital.

Justin and Dante were naked, as well as the women. "I do think," Justin Perry said thoughtfully, "that this is just about as close to total madness as we have ever come."

Raising his head from the white-sheeted massage table three feet away from Justin's, Bob Dante looked over at his friend and grinned. The exquisite brunette was doing marvelous things to Justin's groin with great globs of perfumed oil. Dante knew what Justin was talking about, but he preferred to be facetious. "I'd hardly think," he drawled, "that getting jerked off by a woman would be enough to drive you mad, old cock."

"No, I wouldn't think so," Justin Perry said. And he closed his eyes, driving himself into his own thoughts. There were times when it didn't pay to appeal to the speculative side of Bob Dante; especially not in a situation like this, where Bob was being worked on by the big-tit blonde with the gorgeous body and the loudly lapping mouth.

The subject of madness had been very much on the Old Man's mind—the Old Man being chief of the CIA's Special Assignments Division—during almost all of the past year. The Old Man was Justin and Dante's boss, directing them in elaborate plans that included organized murder against the nation's enemies. But during almost all of the past year, the Old Man had been concerned about madness as a national psychosis. To that end, he had assigned Justin Perry, posing as a psychiatrist, to the staff of the Riverview Sanatarium, in Riverview, Illinois, for a month-long period. Justin's assignment: to study the mad; word had filtered into the Special Assignments Division that something diabolical was afoot at the Riverview Sanatarium, and that whatever the plot was, it might very seriously affect national security.

"That's pretty slim information, isn't it?" Justin had asked the Old Man. He thought he could pose as a psychiatrist well enough—most of them seemed to be involved in a lot of bullshit and double-talk—but the idea of being in a madhouse for as long as a month alarmed him. "Any more clues as to exactly what this plot might be?"

Grim-jawed, precise in every detail, the Old Man had just turned forty. But the job of directing the nation's assassins for the past ten years had taken a harsh toll. His thin face still held its ruggedness, but there were lines now. His brown hair showed traces of gray. But his light blue eyes were filled with the same old determination as he planted Justin with a somber gaze.

"There are no more clues," he said, in such an offhand way that Justin knew he was not telling the truth. Not lying exactly, but withholding information that might be best left to ferment and to age while Justin completed the first part of the operation.

"All right," Justin said, picking up the assignment folder. In many respects, he would find out, as he studied it, that it had the overtones of a theatrical script—a carefully computerized plan of action based on fact and probability, with Justin Perry functioning inside of it as actor, director, and sometimes villain to his own hero— sometimes a very chancy business, indeed, as the CIA followed often labyrinthine trails down dark passages to trap the nation's enemies. "I'm off to Riverview," he said, trying not to show his disappointment.

A goddamned madhouse! Fuck, he felt half crazy himself, most of the time. Suppose they caught him there in Riverview—suppose *they found him out,* and kept him there forever? It was hardly a pleasant thought. "Who's working with me on this?" he asked.

"Bob Dante. He's flying in from Rome this afternoon. You'll see in the assignment sheet at just what point he'll come in."

The Old Man stepped from behind the desk and shook Justin's hand warmly, clapping him on the shoulder at the same time. "Good luck, Justin. And do your best, as always. Things might be shaky now, but they'll come together, as they usually do. Remember, you're not our best agent for nothing."

Justin grinned, some of the tension leaving him. "Sure, Boss. I'll be in touch." And he walked out of the building at Langley, Virginia, into a mild November morning, lighted by a pale sun that reminded him of a white woman's averted face. He drove to his home in Georgetown, over in Washington, where he packed a bag. Then the servant called a taxi which took Justin to Dulles International Airport.

Less than an hour later, Justin was winging his way to Chicago, where he would rent a car and drive out to the hospital at Riverview, Illinois. Meanwhile, he studied the assignment sheet—actually, there were twelve single-spaced typed pages clamped together—marveling at the brilliant twists, shifts, and turns that flowed from the Old Man's mind, as though he were putting together a mystery novel.

The first item on the first sheet had to do with the Federalist-Liberal party's fund-raising event in New York City several nights ago, where various dishes of rat were eaten. The next item dealt with SADIF's invasion of forty-nine madhouses in Canada, Mexico, and the United States, to carry out with them 615 hopelessly mad inmates.

"While it is not yet clear what the ultimate purpose of this SADIF operation is all about," the Old Man had written, "there is reason to believe that its first phase was not entirely successful. Among other points of interest, the asylum in Riverview was completely overlooked, insofar as we can tell, while an asylum only thirty-five miles away was part of the invasion, and seven extremely dangerous inmates were taken from the high-security ward.

"The coincidence of the SADIF raid on the madhouses and the FLP's rat-eating banquet at the Waldorf-Astoria Hotel taking place on the same date does not seem to be accidental. There is not, however, sufficient data available at this time to provide a logical tie-in between the two events. But confidential information we have received does indicate that an infiltration of the Riverview institution ought to throw further light on the matter. This, then, is the first step of Operation Orlando."

Smiling, Justin locked away the report in his briefcase

and settled back in his seat. Operation Orlando. The Old Man was an erudite sonofabitch, and sometimes the code names he came up with gave an indication of the kind of thing that his agents were up against. The only Orlando that Justin knew about was a sleepy little city in central Florida—at least, he remembered it as being a sleepy little city—where he had spent part of a summer with an aunt when he was fifteen years old. The only relative with whom Justin still had contact, Aunt Eugenia wrote him witty, chatty letters about four or five times a year, and always sent him a Christmas gift.

It was Friday, November 4, when Justin's flight landed at Chicago's O'Hare Airport. Justin rented a sturdy blue Ford from Avis, bought three ham sandwiches and a large Coke from a lunch counter in the terminal, and then headed out of Chicago, driving toward the broad, flat plains of Central Illinois. Riverview was 175 miles southwest of Chicago on the Mississippi River; it was now 1:55 in the afternoon. Justin expected to arrive at the asylum around sunset.

But for the present, he munched a sandwich, sipped Coke out of a plastic container, and headed south on the excellent highway out of Evanston. The traffic was light, and there was a brisk wind blowing across the open fields, where crows and other birds congregated. The wheat harvest had been tucked in, and the whole countryside seemed to be permeated with the dry perfumes of fall, the land drawing in on itself, preparing for a heavy winter. Wheeling westward, the sun was to Justin's right, splotched and mottled like a weak egg yolk. He drove with a sense of pleasure, the Ford responding to his slightest touch like a woman responding to sex.

As for his own sex, Justin was conscious of a light erection nestling comfortably in his groin. It had been several weeks since he'd fucked—in a massive orgy with

7

some girls from the Agency, with Bob Dante also in attendance—and he contemplated his next sexual encounter with a sense of mounting excitement. He knew that he was attractive to all kinds of women, and he was thinking about how it would feel to stick his long, thick dick into the woman truck driver—she was right on his ass, in the same lane—who'd been flirting with him since they'd hooked up together a few miles outside of Evanston.

She drove a ten-ton panel Chevrolet truck that was full of bright orange pumpkins, and she handled the outfit with consummate ease. Any women's libber would have been proud of her. Justin wasn't a male chauvinist pig—he honestly thought that women deserved equal rights and ought to have them, as long as they still wanted dick.

He wanted the woman truck driver to have his big dick. And she obviously wanted it. She had winked at him once, her broad red lips parting in a sensual smile that was openly inviting. She was a very pretty brunette. Very good breasts too, from what he'd been able to see at his angle from the truck. Easing his foot down on the accelerator, he sent the speedometer sliding up to ninety. The woman stayed right on his tail. His dick jumped full hard, swelling like a heated snake, and he spread his legs further apart to accommodate its length. He could picture the woman, naked and legs open, sprawling to receive him on the pile of orange pumpkins.

Now in his thirty-sixth year, Justin was an inch over six feet tall, with the slender, disciplined body of a trained athlete. He was inordinately handsome, with regular features, a slab jaw, and broad red lips that seemed to invite a kiss or a cunt. The hair on his head was thick, coarse, and almost blue black, matching the color and texture of his eyebrows, which formed a continuous line across his broad forehead. He had deep-set, dark blue eyes that usually held a mocking smile, as though he invited the whole world, somewhat flamboyantly, to suck him off. This observation had come from a skinny, red-haired Florida girl named Thelma the last summer he'd spent with his Aunt Eugenia in Orlando.

"You don't even know me!" he'd cried; at fifteen, he'd been something of a prude, certainly very easily shocked by someone as honest as Thelma Carew. "How can you say such a thing about me?"

She was hardly more than fifteen herself—"A smart woman don't never tell her age," she'd observed to Justin, when he'd asked her—a real stick of a country girl with extraordinarily beautiful brown eyes, white teeth, and large breasts that swirled around sometimes in her flowered blouses like live melons. Like everybody else in Orlando, with the definite exception of his Aunt Eugenia, Thelma talked like she always had snot in her nose and carried around wads of cotton in her mouth.

"You know what you're saying to the world, dumb boy? You're saying to the world, 'Fuck all of you. And please suck my dick.' That's what you're saying to the world, all right. I ain't never known a dumb white boy like you before, inviting everybody to suck his dick."

He'd been completely shocked. Not that she'd read him so correctly, but that she had the nerve to tell him what she thought. Growing up with his mother and father in Washington, D.C., in the stylized pretensions of George-town, he'd found that the deepest emotions were rarely expressed. It was always a question of "people like us," his mother warned him, leaving him in the dark about people *not* like them. People who turned out to be, on analysis, exactly the kind of people he enjoyed being with. Like the fat-breasted German cook at the Georgetown mansion, who jerked him off in the pantry with astonishing regularity, and sometimes allowed him to shoot off inside of her if she was in a good mood or if he had been "a good boy," as she put it. Sometimes when she sucked him, he felt like she was dragging his guts out through his dick, it was that good, and that painful.

There were also some of the women he got to know outside of the George Washington Military Academy in the rolling hills of Virginia—it was said that George Washington slept there, although it was not said with whom—which Justin had attended since he was twelve. Everybody was banging the dean's daughter, a real blue-eyed slut with stringy blond hair. The dean's wife was also getting her share from some of the ramrod-straight young instructors, it was said. And even the commanding general was said to be getting his share of dick—this slander, if it was that, came from the country whores who congregated outside the drill grounds, like so many pieces of litter in their Sears & Roebuck dresses, black girls and white girls alike, to help the cadets get off there in the willow grove where George Washington was said to have had a vision before going on to Valley Forge to freeze his ass off.

And then there was skinny, red-haired Thelma and the credible crew she commanded that prickly hot summer in Orlando, Florida, when Justin's bitch of a mother had decided to "do" the Riviera without a fifteen-year-old son clumping along with her, as she said, to undo the lie that she was under thirty and still virgin—the latter part being her own lie, which was usually too late to disprove with some young, dumb European dick quivering on the crater rim of her vagina.

But it was Thelma Carew who had been Justin's real black beast from that very day when she backed him up against Aunt Eugenia's kitchen wall and slid a yard of hot, slick tongue down his surprised throat. Except for the extreme pleasure he had felt and the slime of peppermint coating her tongue, he might have thought that he was being kissed by a cow, Thelma's sweet tongue was that long.

Her bony hands slithered like large tarantulas down his heaving chest to his belly and his groin and wrapped around his dick like steel bands. "Lord help me," she said, surprised. "You got a dick just like a nigger. I certainly want that up in me."

He had to squeeze his butt shut to keep from coming. But the excitement was too great anyway, and he broke away, feeling like he ought to run for help, except that his legs were too weak to move. Also, the weight of his dick would have been a burden—"You got a dick just like a nigger," she breathed, biting him through his pants; it was the nicest compliment he'd ever had—like a man trying to run with a sack of potatoes down between his legs.

But he did manage to break away, and Thelma snatched him back again and made that surprising comment about his inviting the whole world to suck him off.

"I certainly don't know what you mean by that," he'd said. In those days, he had a slight Virginia accent, and he must have sounded to Thelma like a little southern girl.

"Why don't you come off that shit, dumb boy?" Her hot breath snorting through her flared nostrils seemed to scald him. He backed away, but the wooden wall held him.

I'm going to shoot in a minute, he thought. But he said, "Why don't you come off yours?"

"All you dumb northern white boys want to be sucked off," she pontificated. "They scared of getting me pregnant, that's why they let me eat their come. Also, it's a mother fixation."

He was so surprised that he laughed and felt completely at ease. Also, his blue eyes narrowed with dark pleasure as Thelma fell to her knees on the floor in front of him, working frantically at his zipper. She indeed ate his come, right down to the last drop; but what he'd really wanted to do was to fuck.

Still, her comment about the pleasure he got from oral sex and his so-called "mother fixation"—how very easily she'd condemned the entire male part of the white race, he'd thought—did not escape him so easily. If he did, as she said, have a dick like a nigger—and the black boys at the academy told him the same thing when he jacked off with them in the shower—then it ought to have followed that there was something other than his dick that was unredeemably niggerish about him. But in his own examinations of himself, he was simply a "white" boy, with designs on neither the white race nor the black. He liked poetry, sports, music, history, and any hole he could fit his dick into. In moments of great need, he'd been known to fuck the ground or the opening left after taking a piece of lightwood out of a pine tree. In his own estimation, he was "universal," stressing the dictionary's apt definition of an indivisible whole, given or extended to all.

Which of course got him into enormous trouble with his mother, who had a surprisingly narrow view about everybody and everything, as immutable in her blatant stupidity as base metal. Even at fifteen, he cringed at her narrowness from behind the constantly shifting barrier of his own amplitude. She liked peanut brittle, among other aberrations, and kept it all over the house, like little puddles of brown shit thrust by untrained puppies into cut-glass dishes by Tiffany. All of her millions—the money was hers; Justin's father was an air-force general, and used his position to stay as far away from the woman as possible—all her millions had not taught her the basic decencies of clear thinking and polite speech.

Hannah, the cook, was "that Kraut." The black servant emerged as "our nigger." The president of the United States, whom she frequently entertained at the Georgetown mansion, was "that asshole in the Oval Office." It was more inappropriate than it was startling to hear such filth drip from carefully painted lips into the garbage can of her general conversation.

She did manage, however, to control herself when there were people of importance around, for she was an inveterate social climber. A stunning platinum blonde, with the almost immobile features of a beautiful corpse, she was considered one of Washington's top hostesses; and the tenacity with which society titles stick was proven by the fact that everyone in Washington—from Justin, to his father, to the asshole president of the United States—knew that she was sucking off the chauffeur, and was still able to retain her title as society hostess. It did not occur to Justin that she was mad, this woman he called his mother, until after she had died brutally at the hand of Justin's father. Since then, he'd sometimes felt very dubious about his sanity, blood strains being what they are.

But it was that summer in Orlando, Florida, under the hot hands, lips, and between the thighs of Thelma Carew, that gave Justin his best opportunity to express his universality and extend himself to all. Aunt Eugenia was an excellent, elderly woman of the most perfect breeding. She treated Justin with an ample amount of satisfying love and then left him to his own devices as she went peacefully about her own life, usually out of the house.

Thelma, who worked part-time for Aunt Eugenia, was usually in the house. Thelma also had a gang, which included four other white girls, and two boys, one black and one white, who acted as flunkies, and sometimes put on a show by stripping naked and jerking and sucking each other off under the baleful eyes of the penis-envying girls. When this sort of thing happened at Aunt Eugenia's, Thelma spread copies of the *Orlando Times* to keep the boys' come off the living-room rug, if the girls didn't drink it. It was this gang, Thelma announced to Justin one night in his bedroom, that had decided to sacrifice a white person to the spirit of things past.

"You know all that's happening in the South today?" she whispered, although she might have bellowed, or even talked in a normal voice. Aunt Eugenia slept downstairs in the opposite end of the house, leaving Justin to his privacy in an upstairs bedroom. There was even an oak tree outside very close to the window, which he could shinny up and down when the spell was upon him. Aunt Eugenia had obviously read Mark Twain and knew that the best way to treat teenage boys in the summertime is to provide them with oak trees to climb up and down and lots of casual love and guaranteed privacy.

"You know what's happening in the South today?" Thelma whispered. "Well, we've decided that somebody white ought to be *sacrificed*, and that'll make everything all right."

Justin indeed did not know what was going on in the South—the sit-ins, garbage collector strikes, Martin Luther King, and the whole varied panorama of the sixties' civil rights movement—but he was sure that Thelma was right in what she said. She gave him so much pleasure throughout his whole being. She had taught him to *fuck*—not the mere appearance of fucking—but how to grind down deep and dirty inside her, his narrow ass spinning with the most marvelous pleasure, almost casually, while his heart ran a mile a minute and the nerves in his dick did giddy handsprings.

She had taught him to kiss dirty, to talk dirty, to eat pussy without gagging at the sometimes sardine smell, and to mash flies with his bare hands without even flinching. Thelma indeed was a revelation; and if her gang, of which she was chairperson—the word was Thelma's, later stolen by the womens' libbers; meaning that she was all things to her gang—if Thelma thought that a white person needed to be sacrificed for civil rights, then Justin thought so too.

"Who do you have in mind?" Justin said.

"You, dumb boy."

She'd been sitting on his dick, her tight legs locked backward along his thighs. He was so surprised that his dick shriveled up inside her.

"Me?" He also felt terrible betrayal; it was the first time she'd called him "dumb boy" in five weeks and three days. "Why do you want to sacrifice me?"

"Because you're a white boy." She treated him as though she was not a "white" girl.

"I . . . I thought you didn't see me that way anymore."

"What way do you think I see you? Like you're a white girl?"

That disgusted him. He shoved her carefully away, went to the bathroom, and stepped under the cold water, soaping himself.

Thelma talked to him through the curtain. "I'm sorry I said that." She did sound contrite, although her mouth was full of cornflakes and blueberries and cold milk, which they'd brought from the kitchen. "You ain't hardly no girl, that pistol you got hanging between your legs."

That pleased him—he got half a hard-on, even under the cold water—but not enough to want to be sacrificed.

"What about my aunt?" he said.

Thelma laughed. "She ain't got no pistol."

"I know that. I mean, for the sacrifice." He liked Aunt Eugenia, but he liked himself better.

Again Thelma laughed. "I know what you mean. You ought to be ashamed of yourself, wanting to sacrifice somebody as nice as your aunt is. Besides, she ain't got no pistol."

"Why would she need one?"

"She don't. But our sacrifice do. It's got to be somebody white and somebody just like you, with a pistol just like yours.''

She pulled aside the shower curtain and stepped in with him. Cornflakes hung at the corners of her lips, and he thought that was really sexy.

''You and your mother fixation,'' she said darkly. ''You want me to suck you off, don't you? Then you've got to ask, dumb boy. You've got to *beg*.''

''Suck me,'' he said weakly. ''Oh, please suck me!''

But she was already gobbling him. And he knew with dire certainty that he would be her sacrifice.

He felt the milk churning in his big balls; he couldn't stand it any longer.

He slowed, angling the Ford off the highway onto the shoulder. A flock of birds in the empty field rose up in a scattered cloud and flapped away, squawking. He remembered the time he'd fucked Thelma out in a field somewhat like this one, her red hair pillowed on a dark green watermelon.

''Hurt me! *Hurt me!*'' she huffed. He tried to drive his dick right through her. She doubled up against him, gasping with pleasure. ''Oh . . . that's good . . . That's so motherfucking *good* . . . !'' The black boy who jerked off the white one taught them all the very dirtiest nigger words, and they all knew about mother-fucking. Afterwards, he and Thelma busted open the watermelon and ate it with their bare hands.

Now, he got out of the car and half limped down into the field. Looking back over his shoulder, he saw the girl bring the truck to a stop behind the Ford. He knew that she was coming to him.

Suddenly, the sun seemed to blind him. He opened his pants, pulled down the zipper, and waited.

He heard her get down from the truck, the cabin door slam. "Anything I can do to help you?" she called. She had a sweet, musical voice; something about it stirred another faraway memory.

Twisting toward her, he took out his dick, all nine-and-a-half inches of it coming out like a thick, angry-looking hose. Her eyes seemed to widen in surprise and pleasure. She was small, well built, in a pair of blue fashion designer coveralls and small, brown, bootlike shoes that made her look cute.

"Right here?" she said.

"Right here," he growled. Goddamn, but he *needed* her. Besides, he worked for the United States government, *killed* for the government. What could anybody do to him?

He snaked out his arm and jabbed a commanding finger at the ground, as though ordering a dog to heel. She came toward him in a rush and kneeled. . . .

Afterwards, he said, "God, I needed that," not without wondering again about his own madness. They had been pretty well hidden from the highway by the bulk of their own vehicles. And the traffic along here, approaching the tollgate to Riverview, was very light. Still, he'd caught glimpses of surprised farmers, who slowed down, then speeded up again, fleeing from the fact of evil. It only excited him more.

The girl laughed, stepping away. "I'd sure like to enjoy that under more orthodox conditions," she said. "Where are you headed to?"

"Riverview," he said. "Just on the other side of the tollbooth. We can stop there, if you'd like."

She had enormous brown eyes and a very greedy mouth. He wondered what her pussy was like. "We'll stop there," she said. She went back to the truck, swinging her ass, a pretty-looking little boy-girl in that outfit. He went back to the Ford; he felt a lot better now, at least in one respect.

*   *   *

The sacrifice with Thelma's gang had gone unexpectedly well. Aunt Eugenia's living room was apparently too limited for such an important event. So, on the night of the affair, Thelma showed up in a grisly old peeling gray Model-T Ford with the rest of her entourage stuffed like so many satchels into the back. The front seat beside her was reserved for Justin, the victim of honor, with a broken spring in the seat exactly placed to poke him in the ass. Thelma drove away with great verve from Aunt Eugenia's white clapboard house, down Compton Street, across the tracks, and into Niggertown, where she made two or three rowdy swings through the neighborhood, just to show off that anybody like her could drive without a license and with very few lessons. Finally, they hit the dirt road that took them out to Lake Kinoshee, where the full moon was just rising from the water like a golden lady leaving her bath. Thelma and her club piled out at once, but Justin had sat there trying to collect his scattered feelings.

Were they going to kill him? Reasonably, it was the first thought to come to mind when anybody talked about sacrifice. In the past week, since the decision had been made, he'd wanted to ask Thelma a dozen times but had not because he was terrified that she'd screw up her face and answer him quite truthfully in the affirmative.

He was miserable all that week. And even Aunt Eugenia, that most splendid of people, made a discreet inquiry or two about his health and even felt his forehead for a fever. But at his weak protests that he was fine, she withdrew back across to her side of the loving gulf that separated them, waiting if he called out but still prepared to give immediate aid if he didn't and she saw his safety jeopardized in the least by his stubbornness. In her role as sister to Justin's father, she imitated to perfection the general's complete understanding of an adolescent's summer vaca-

18

tion needs, and she was prepared to let Justin twist and turn inside the torments of his own freedom, as all intelligent people must do, until new crises arise to dislodge and replace the old ones.

As for Justin's own thoughts about the possibility of his actually being sacrificed by Thelma and her bunch, it seemed to be a bloody mess. He'd gone to the library and read his way through several sections in anthropological studies that had to do with human sacrifice in the Old and New Worlds. The bloodiest ones in this part of the continent appeared to have taken place in middle America. In Mexico alone, the Spaniards who came to conquer Montezuma walked upon floors some several feet deep from the accumulation of dried blood from so many human sacrifices. One report had it that on the tops of their pyramids the Aztecs with obsidian knives ripped out quivering hearts and the complete genitals from young men who had been especially prepared for the honor.

At the same time, Justin found other information about human sacrifices that puzzled him at first. Cortez and his men came across sacrificial victims being fattened up for the event in bamboo cages. The Spaniards opened the doors of the cages, setting the victims free, but they had to prod them with sticks to make the victims come out.

"You're free!'" The Catholic priests cried, speaking through interpreters. But the Indians slunk away and went back into the cages.

Again they were prodded out; again they went back inside. Until the cages were burned, and some of the victims wept in bitter disappointment. Of course, the Spaniards did not understand.

Justin did not understand either. Yet, watching Thelma and her gang lined up like cross-legged blackbirds, sitting at a distance from the lakeshore where the water resembled a great puddle of gold reflecting the moon within its depths, he felt a sudden and important surge of his own importance to all of humanity—or even to such a tattered part of it that Thelma and her gang represented. He felt no fear. Or, to turn it around, he felt the first onset of bravery. The Indians had not feared their cages; he would not fear them either.

"I am ready for the sacrifice," he said, in a strong, new voice.

Thelma turned and smiled. They had been sitting like monkeys in a row, watching the white gulls come in, silhouetted against the moon like the small burnished ships of Vikings floating on waves of light.

"Take your clothes off," Thelma said.

It was an order to everybody, and they all stood up and undressed in the heat. For the first time, Justin saw that there was another white girl among them. She was so grimy herself that he could tell her race accurately only by her stringy hair.

"That's Betty," Thelma said. "She's visiting Orlando from somewhere in Illinois."

Justin nodded formally at the two strong eyes peering at him from between the rat tails of hair. He could see the funny-looking conjunction of her legs in a carved V; her breasts were small and barely formed, more like two dirt stains on her chest. And it was surprising how clear the night was, as though day overlaid the darkness in stark white designs. Of course, the moon helped too, showing the girl's face with the sharply pointed chin when she pushed her hair back.

"I eat worms," she said dramatically. From her voice, he figured that she was about two or even three years younger than he was. But there was a sadness in her voice, as though she condemned herself.

"Why do you eat worms?" Justin said.

She shrugged thin shoulders. "I *like* worms . . . dirt . . . anything filthy."

"It's called *scatological*," Thelma Carew said knowledgeably. "She even eats shit."

"I do not, either," the girl said, trying to withdraw behind two thin arms crossed over her chest. "Besides, worms are full of protein."

"So is shit," Thelma grunted, and turned to Justin. "Anyway, dumb boy, *this* is your sacrifice. All you got to do is fuck her. Then everything's going to be all right in the South again."

He felt stupidly relieved. How had he ever thought that they intended to sacrifice him in that bloody way?

Then, understanding swept him at once—he'd been thinking that he'd fuck Betty but wouldn't kiss her—and his dick suddenly sprang up and nearly touched her belly.

"Are you a virgin?" he asked her.

"Yes." She took a step away, as though alarmed at the size of him. But she sounded shy, as though pleased that he could be so astute.

"Of course she's a virgin," Thelma cut in strongly. "That's why she's a sacrifice. Whoever heard of anybody sacrificing an old whore?" She pronounced the word to rhyme with *hoe*. "Now, you all get up there on the front end of the car. That'll have to make do as an altar. I can see that Peterman's knife is all ready."

Then she turned to Betty with a baleful stare; in the moonlight, her eyes suddenly walled like a horse's. "You just better make sure there's a lot of blood," she said. But her voice sounded full of bitterness and perhaps even nostalgia, perhaps even doubts, about Betty's purity. And there was sadness too, as though she condemned herself.

Justin and Betty climbed up on the car hood while Thelma rallied her troops, and the six of them clumped and whooped around the car like drunken Indians. Justin

21

completely mistrusted the ceremony—he was convinced
that it was something that Thelma had made up on the
spot—but he was pleased at Betty's thin, bony shyness as
she curled in his arms like a kind of living flower. Her
sharp lips nibbled at his neck like minnows.

"Please don't shoot in me," she said. "I'm afraid of
getting pregnant."

He was afraid of making her pregnant. "I won't," he
said.

It was all quite new to him. He'd never had a virgin
before, and he'd certainly never had to withdraw from a
girl before. But he handled it with an amazing degree of
skill, considering his lack of experience. Also, the impro-
vised altar was precarious and uncomfortable; they kept
sliding earthward until he learned how to anchor them to
the slick top with the adhesiveness of his bare feet. Round
and round them, Thelma and her gang bumped in a circle,
singing something that sounded like a song about bubble
gum.

Of course, Betty helped him too. She strained up against
him with her almost boyish body, guiding him in, impal-
ing herself on him with surprising energy, as though he
was taking away from her something that she despised, a
surgeon cutting out an annoying sore.

"Ahhhhhh!" she cried.

Her arms flew back, grabbing a part of the windshield
for support. He felt the figurehead of a stallion on the car
front bite into his leg. As his dick moved into her, he
thought of the watermelon that he and Thelma had eaten in
the field with their hands. Opening his eyes, he saw
Thelma gazing at him, then down into the girl's face. "It
is done," Themla said, in sepulchral tones. "You all can
climb on down now. I got to get this car back to my
cousin." It was difficult not to notice the anger, even the
jealousy, in her voice.

Justin and Betty took their clothes and bounded down to the lake to repair themselves, touching sometimes very shyly in the ice-cold water. "I'll never forget you," Betty promised him. He felt good about that, almost gallant. "I'll never forget you either," he said. He stepped through the water to her and held her incredibly skinny body against his. The frightening sperm had spent itself on the car hood, although it had cost him a supreme effort to withdraw from her. He saw that the moon had turned blood red. Gulls floated on the lake with their beaks drawn against their breasts, like disgruntled miniature men.

He never went back to Orlando after that. As he turned tall and strikingly handsome, his mother suddenly discovered him as a social asset. If she did not keep him in Georgetown to be photographed with her—he was still young enough for her not to feel old, and old enough for some people to think that he might be her lover rather than her son—she shipped him off to exotic places or to spend the summer with his father, an air-force general, making sure that the gossip columnists got the news.

He never saw Betty again after that first time. Thelma said that she had gone back to Illinois a few days after the sacrifice. Did she really eat worms? Justin wondered. He'd looked up the word *scatological* and found that Thelma had been only partly right. He thought about Betty a lot for many years after that, with a sense of fondness and even sacrifice; if he had been her first dick, she had been his first virgin.

As for Thelma Carew, it seemed that something subtle but profound had happened to her. For the rest of that summer, she called him Peterman—the *peter* man—and he liked that. But he saw that something in their relationship had changed now when she came to his room. No more shinnying up the oak tree like a boy. She walked through the front door, however quietly. She wore clean dresses

23

instead of faded, dirty old jeans, and touched his arm with unaccustomed tenderness as he ate cornflakes with plump Florida blueberries and ice-cold milk. If Justin had not exactly become a man, the summer had made Thelma into an ambitious woman. One of the last times that he was with her, she told him that she had decided to become a doctor.

As for the efficacy of the sacrifice performed on the altar of the Model-T Ford, the South continued to be convulsed by civil rights activists, and the movement took on alarming overtones of violence that threatened to divide the nation in a new kind of civil war. Justin began reading the newspapers religiously—years later, he would take his degree in journalism and communications arts from Syracuse University—and came to conclude that Thelma's pronouncements about a sacrifice to the spirit of things past had probably been a lot of bullshit.

As for the spirit of things present, he saw the change in Thelma and felt some of it in himself and even in Aunt Eugenia. She seemed convinced that the summer had been a success, for herself as well as for Justin. "Thank you so much for coming," she said to him at the bus station. They shook hands quite formally. It was one of the many things he liked about her, that she didn't slobber over him like other female relatives did.

She was a very handsome woman of small proportions but of large comprehension. Any other woman—his mother, for example—would have stood guard at the house door, so many goings-on between himself and Thelma. "Aunt Eugenia . . ." He felt the need to confess something to her.

"Yes, dear?"

"I want you to know that I think you are a very great person. And I thank you so very much for inviting me, and for putting up with me in your home."

She was splendid in her reaction. "I think that you are also a very great person, Justin. So we rather deserve each other, don't we?" She touched his arm, with a little laugh. "Now, there's your bus. I shall write you from time to time. But don't bother too much about responding if you find yourself too busy with other things. And be sure to give my very best regards to your parents."

"Yes, Aunt Eugenia." He almost felt like crying. He hugged her quickly, and very hard. Her body felt so fragile in his arms. Then he climbed on the bus. She waved as it pulled off.

He was aware that the summer had helped him to shed the skin of childhood, although it would be many years before he would take on the complexion of a man. That would come later, after college, and service in Vietnam, after his marriage to Bambi and the birth of their son, then Bambi's death. And then the horrifying revelation that the woman he'd called his mother all those years was not really his mother at all.

The woman masquerading as his mother had been a key agent of SADIF, the Sons and Daughters in Freedom. And so had Justin's father, although it became clear that the woman had been the fierce, manipulating power. They'd arranged the death of Justin's wife Bambi, after Bambi had discovered that they were tampering with computers of the Air Defense Command, faking the penetration of Russian aircraft into American airspace in order to set up a clamor at home for higher defense spending.

While Justin had been shocked that they could have so cold-bloodedly engineered the death of his wife, he had been devastated by the confession that the woman had not been his mother. He would never forget the biting scorn of her words as she told him. "You are not my son," she said spitefully. "You were already born when I married your father. I promised him never to tell you. But if you're going to carry on this way, then you ought to know. *I am not your mother!* You are obviously the spawn of some whore he'd known before he met me. I was generous enough to accept you, and to raise you as my son. It has not always been pleasant, believe me." Her hands flew dramatically to her breasts. "I am *not* your mother! God, what a relief to be able to say it after all these years. *I am not your mother!*"

Sometime during that night of horror, Justin's father had shot the mocking woman, then killed himself. After Justin had recovered somewhat from the slaughter, he had called Aunt Eugenia on the telephone.

"Yes, I've heard the sad news," she said, with careful composure. "It was on the late night news. I was thunderstruck, to tell the truth. Your poor father. But how are you, dear? And little Roger? Is there anything I can do? I know that it must be a terrible time for you."

It was comforting to hear her carefully controlled voice, although he could tell that she had been crying. "No, Aunt Eugenia. I think everything will be all right on this end. But how about you? Do you want me to come there? Or will you come here?"

"I'll be all right," she said. "Now that I know that you and the boy are out of danger. Look after him. And yourself too. I'll always be here if you need me."

"You are so great, Aunt Eugenia! Absolutely great! I want you to know that I love you very much. Father did too. Whatever this mess was that he got involved in, was not his fault." He did not want to complicate matters by telling her that he had suddenly found out that he was a bastard, certainly not to sully his father's memory, her beloved brother.

"I love you too, my dear. And give my love to little Roger. It will of course take time for all of us to get over this. But time has a way of healing."

So the bonds between Justin and his aunt were very strong. He went into the Central Intelligence Agency's Special Assignments Division—also known as the Death Squad—without telling her, although he sometimes suspected that she knew. He exchanged letters with her, and presents at Christmas.

And now, years later, he had become the CIA's top killer and was on his way now to masquerade as a psychiatrist in a madhouse, where all indications seemed to be that mayhem was about to be spawned. And he was still relentlessly on the trail of SADIF, exacting bloody vengeance for what it had done to his father, and to his wife, and to himself.

TWO

Heated with excitement from thinking about the old days, some of it brought to mind by the Old Man's assignment sheet on Operation Orlando, Justin Perry looked into the rearview mirror and saw with satisfaction that the girl driving the truck with the pumpkins was still behind him. And for a few minutes, he felt a sense of sorrow at the dreadful deceptiveness and even the predictable inevitability of human nature.

So much like in the nursery rhyme: the rat eats the cheese, and the cat eats the rat—layer after layer of despicable energy involved in the wasteful act of devouring. Some people would call it life. Until we find ourselves trussed with an apple up our asses, dressed with spices and everything nice on the platter of God, when some would call by its other name, death. Sneaky and deceptive, God and death, sometimes masquerading as beauty.

To ease his thoughts, he shook himself like a wet dog shaking off water. Remembering Thelma and the so-called sacrifice had made him somber. But now he felt a sense of exhilaration as he saw the two-lane tollbooth farther ahead at the exit to Riverview. There were two guards on duty to collect tolls for both directions.

As Justin prepared to slow down, he saw that he and the girl behind him in the truck were the only traffic approaching in the southbound lane. The northbound side was completely free of traffic; the guard from the booth on that side had come over and seemed to be talking pleasantly to the guard covering this lane.

Justin had just started to brake completely, digging into his pocket for coins, every sense alert, when he heard the sudden rapid racing of the truck motor behind him. Snapping his head around, he saw the truck bearing down on him. The girl's face behind the wheel was twisted in a hideous smile.

Slamming his foot on the accelerator, Justin sent the Ford shuddering forward. At the same time, he saw that the two uniformed guards in the tollbooth had drawn guns. A bullet slammed into the windshield, shattering it. Justin cursed silently, twisting the steering wheel to the left as he threw the Ford into reverse.

It collided heavily with the oncoming truck, before he shifted to a fast first, sending the Ford spinnning away drunkenly from the truck and to the left side of the highway, into the northbound lane.

He heard the sharp *ping* of more bullets as he half-crouched over the wheel, keeping the car at a protective angle from the guards and their guns. For some reason, they were shooting wildly, not even bothering to take aim.

A grim smile crossed his lips as he saw the truck lurch into the lane between the tollbooths. The girl had apparently lost control, probably from excitement. Well, he thought, that's too fucking bad. Women's lib wouldn't be so proud of her after all.

And what a pity, he thought, because she did give good head. But even as he thought, he had raced the motor; and now he sent the Ford leaping across the highway like a battering ram and braced himself for the impact as the Ford crashed into the driver's side of the truck. He heard the girl scream as the guards' guns barked simultaneously.

He'd better get the hell out of here, he thought. Again he sent the Ford grinding backward. But the motor sputtered, and stopped. Moving in a flash, he grabbed his briefcase, opened the door, and fell into a football roll onto the asphalt highway. He came up with his .38 Colt Special revolver in his right hand.

He saw the guards working furiously at the truck door, on the side where the girl sat. The other side of the truck was mashed up against the tollbooth. And on this side, the impact from Justin's car had effectively jammed the door. The girl was trapped inside the truck. She was trying to get out through the window. He saw terrible agony twisting her face.

Maybe I ought to shoot her, he thought. But it was only a fleeting thought, nothing serious. He was far from feeling humane. The same thing was probably true of the guards; for they seemed to have given up on trying to get the girl out of the truck and were fighting like hell to get away.

Justin sprinted across the highway, took a long dive into the wheat field, landing hard on his shoulder. And was up and running as the explosion from behind knocked him ten feet, as though he had been slammed in the back by an evil hand. He counted slowly to five, then stood up, and turned.

The tollbooth, the truck, and the Avis car were all a flaming mess. He saw nothing of the guards or the girl. But he did see that the highway was spattered with pieces of pumpkins for fifty feet on both sides of where the tollbooths had stood. What a waste of good Thanksgiving pie, he thought. He wondered how much dynamite SADIF had put under the pumpkins.

And the girl, dumb bitch. She'd obviously activated the detonator before trying to ram Justin's car in the lane. And then got herself rammed good, and trapped inside the truck, and had died for being dumb. A real waste of good pussy, Justin thought. If she had waited until they'd fucked in the Riverview Hotel before she'd tried to knock him off, she might have succeeded.

The highway in both directions was remarkably free of traffic as he brushed himself off and began walking, swinging his briefcase jauntily against his right leg. He knew that the Old Man's assignment sheets were safe in the briefcase. And that among several 8×10-inch glossy photographs attached to the sheet, one was of the girl who had just blown herself and her SADIF cohorts to kingdom come.

He recalled the neatly typed notation attached to the back of the photograph: *Carla Strickland, SADIF agent, age 32; b. Chicago, IL, 1/4/51. Joined SADIF 3/7/79. Expert in demolitions. Extremely dangerous; approach with caution. Possible tail out of Chicago.*

Justin smiled at the Old Man's unintended pun. He felt just fine, walking along the deserted highway. No, not so deserted. A sleek blue Ford LTD was approaching on the other side in the northbound lane. Justin was heading south, and didn't even bother to look up when the car pulled to a stop on the other side of the highway.

A man stuck his head out of the window and called. "I thought I heard an explosion," he said. "Did something happen up the road?"

"Nothing very exciting," Justin said, and walked on. The car took off, and Justin kept walking south. He felt just fine. The Old Man's assignment sheets sometimes impressed him as being absolute works of art. None of them ever knew where the Old Man got his advance information about what might be in store for them.

But it rarely failed to pay off. It was like walking onto a movie set and making the thing work out as it ought to by the simple fact of your being there yourself. The script was well written, Justin thought, but certainly not so rigid that you got the feeling of being a puppet. There was a lot of room to move around inside of—to improvise, edit, rewrite—as the forces of SADIF heard the bell and converged like mad dogs on the CIA's possible victim.

And that was what made it really exciting, Justin thought. SADIF obviously also had its assignment sheets, its agents briefed with facts, alerted for probabilities, actors from the other side of the chessboard, opposing players in a lethal game where checkmate often meant death. . . .

He'd been listening to a car coming behind him. And now he moved to the shoulder and stopped as the car slowed down. Driving the car was the same man who'd yelled at Justin from the other side of the highway. The man behind the wheel was short, plump, balding, around forty-five, wearing horn-rimmed glasses. His photograph was not among those in Justin's briefcase.

"My God!" he cried. "That is really quite something, what happened up there." He squinted through his glasses at Justin. "Do you know what happened back there?"

Justin shrugged. "Afraid not. My car stalled about a mile back. I heard the explosion too. But it was all over by the time I got there." He planted the man with a very arrogant stare. "Are you a cop or something?"

The man smiled, his pale blue eyes seeming to melt. "No, for heavens sake, no. I'm not a cop. I'm Joel Peters, editor of the *Carlton Chronicle*. Carlton's a little town on an island out in the Mississippi. I'm going there now. You want a ride?"

"I'm going to Riverview," Justin said.

"Well, I'll drop you there. I was going to make a report

to the state police barracks there anyway. My civic duty, you know."

Justin got in. Peters seemed a pleasant enough guy, if something of a dud as an editor and a journalist. A good reporter would have been back there at the explosion site, snooping around, trying to make the pieces of the puzzle fit together before the police got there.

He told Peters so, and Peters laughed. "Yes, I suppose you're right," he said. "That might have been true in the old days. But it could be dangerous now. An explosion like that might have something to do with terrorists. And they might still be somewhere around." He peered over at Justin owlishly. "You're not a terrorist, are you?"

"No," Justin said. "I'm a doctor. A psychiatrist. I'm going to join the staff at Riverview Sanatarium."

"Are you now?" Peters sounded inordinately pleased. "I know the director at Riverview Sanatarium. In fact, he's one of my very best friends. Dr. Porter. Dr. Steve Porter." He stuck out a hairy hand, driving with the other. "And what did you say your name was?"

"I didn't," Justin said brusquely. "Do me a favor, will you? Wake me up when we get to Riverview."

He could feel the man's hurt and surprise as he leaned his head back against the seat and closed his eyes. "I'd be more than glad to," Peters said.

A fucking fag, Justin thought. Not the real take-it-in-the-ass, dick-sucking kind, but a fag nevertheless. He gave the impression of being a somewhat fat, soft, well-dressed, perfumed white worm. Anxious for gossip, probably to share with his old mother or a maiden aunt—not a wife, because his kind would always flash the old wedding ring as a symbol of his masculinity, and he wasn't wearing one.

So it was probably back to his mother he was rushing with the juicy gossip about the explosion. He gave the unmistakable impression of still being a mother's boy at his age. She probably chose his clothes for him, and that male gook he was wearing. But it was really his eyes that gave him away; he'd never won a single argument with his mother in his entire life. And he was starved for conversation with even a stranger he'd picked up on the highway.

But the truth was that Justin had no time for making small talk. Slumped in the seat with his eyes closed—although his nerves were taught and steeled for action—he let his mind drift back to a talk he'd heard the Old Man give three years ago to top-level intelligence and counterespionage officials from the United States and its NATO allies.

While the general public had known almost nothing of a major shift in the strategy of intelligence units and counterespionage practices all over the world, the Old Man had been one of the chief architects in this revolutionary change in methodology. "It's getting so that everybody knows how we work," he grumbled. "And what our methods are. Our security measures are so weak and there are so many leaks to the press that our covers are blown almost as soon as we put them into operation. I wonder if any of you is aware of the irony of the U. S. Congress having to approve funds of *covert* CIA operations in El Salvador. To the rest of the world, I am sure that such a thing makes us who work in intelligence appear to be a bunch if incompetent fools."

His strongest criticism went to the American press, and Justin was in complete agreement with him. Not only were former CIA agents writing books about the agency's covert operations, but the press was constantly digging away for sensational revelations that not only put security units in a bad light, but effectively undermined the public's faith in the government and all of its operations.

"The press in the United States is downright irresponsible," the Old Man went on. "Every country, no matter how large or how small, how weak or powerful it may be, engages in covert spying and clandestine operations when such activities have to do with its own national security. We all know that the business of any government on every level is to look out for the best interests of its citizens. In the United States, the government is freely elected, and one supposes that its leaders are honestly concerned with forming a more perfect union, establishing justice, ensuring domestic tranquillity, providing for the common defense, promoting the general welfare, and securing the blessing of liberty to ourselves and our posterity, as the Constitution so succinctly states.

"But we have come to a time now of complete arbitrariness on the part of some of our citizens. The whole thing nowadays seems to be to thumb one's nose at the government, to ridicule it, to strip its every act down to the bare bones, to expose its every kink and wrinkle. No government is perfect, and that of the United States least of all. But it does have honest, dedicated civil servants who are concerned with maintaining our country's strength, which is based on the democratic ideals of justice and equality for all.

"If we have not been able to achieve these ideals, it is primarily because we *are* a democratic society, in the midst of constant flux and change, dealing with multiple personalities which sometimes make democracy impossible to achieve in the short run, because it deals primarily with a consensus of what the majority of the people think.

"But nowadays, what people in America think is generally fed to them and manipulated by the press. And the press has become so powerful, and so irresponsible in its arrogance, that any criticism of it calls forth a great mountain of charges and abuse and muckracking against the person brave enough to criticize it.

"The American press is without control and without scruples. It keeps the country in a constant state of turmoil and agitation. The public does not think anymore; it reacts to fear as served to it by the press, in large chunks of sensationalism twenty-four hours a day. The First Amendment to the Constitution, guaranteeing freedom of the press, could never have envisioned the state of world affairs today. Or how the press would grow to be big business, and a government unto itself.

"As to the public that is created by this state of affairs, it is hostile, arbitrary, ignorant, panic-stricken, and incredibly uninformed. Given such a condition, there is a general reversal of roles, in which no public figure is ever trusted. A man of virtue is immediately thought to be a scoundrel, *because the press says that he is virtuous*. And scoundrels are immediately made into men of virtue *because the press says that he is a scoundrel*!

"And scoundrels are made into heroes, and even become elected officials, because of their constant exposure in the press and because people have become conditioned to believing the exact opposite of whatever it is that the press reports. When we are dealing with today's American public, what we have on our hands is a dangerous mob of sullen, willful children who can be easily manipulated into turning negatives into positives and positives into negatives.

"Given this dangerous and alarming state of affairs, it is essential that we alter our intelligence and counterespionage apparatuses—their initiatives and their responses—in such a way that we may still continue to work for the good of the American people, albeit against their will and certainly against their knowledge. To paraphrase a famous quotation, the best way in the current American climate to ensure the triumph of evil is that good men are said by the press to be *good men*!"

That last part, Justin thought, was a strange way to put the matter. Even dictatorial, authoritarian, and extremely self-serving. All tyrants have insisted that their course of action is best for the people, even when the people are against it.

But in this case, Justin was convinced that the Old Man was right. There was a war going on between two worlds, two ideologies—the good guys and the bad guys, if you will—and a large part of the American people, misusing their freedom and panic-stricken inside their ignorance, were perfectly willing to give away our precious freedoms to the Russians.

Hence, so-called "peace demonstrations" calling for unilateral disarmament, agonized cries against emplacement of long- and short-range missiles in Europe as a deterrent against Russia, the insistence on "human rights" in foreign countries where human rights were never heard of.

These things, naturally, took place only in the Western democracies and only against the United States. In practically no other part of the world—certainly not in communist countries—is there ever a demonstration against Russia. Such demonstrations are not permitted and not needed; the best anti-American work is done by our own citizens. In a dreadful abuse of freedom, Americans are using their constitutional rights to destroy America and to deliver us over to communism.

Greek mythology speaks of Erisichthon, who was a profane person and a despiser of the gods. On one occasion, he felled a venerable oak tree in a grove sacred to the goddess Ceres. Angered at this act, Ceres gave Erisichthon an insatiable appetite, until Erisichthon was finally compelled to eat himself. This, in effect, was what Justin saw happening to the American people, its insatiable appetite for the prerogatives of freedom pushed for commercial gain by the press. We are consuming ourselves, Justin had thought uneasily.

And the Old Man had apparently thought the same thing. The rest of the conference took place behind sealed doors among only the highest-level officials. Again, it was the Old Man who took the podium.

"What we must do," he said, "is to make certain assumptions about the enemy which it has not been really necessary to make before. First of all, we must assume that he knows what we know about him. As for what we *don't* know about him, we must make every effort to find out, whether by honorable or dishonorable acts. Furthermore, we must make drastic changes in our attempts to thwart the efforts of such organizations as SADIF and the KGB to undermine our national strength and our faith in our democratic institutions.

"We may also assume that American citizens, for reasons which are generally erroneous, are as much against our organizations as the enemy is. And our citizens should be treated with the same amount of suspicion and circumspection as we accord our enemies.

"With the anarchy of the press becoming stronger every day, we are in grave danger of falling into the hands of our enemies like a rotten apple falling from a tree. More than anything else, a free press ought to be a responsible press. Its duties are to inform and advise the people, to define issues, to foster discussion, and to act as a watchdog against the *illegitimate* practices of government. It is not illegitimate for the American government to want the very best for the American people.

"As it is, the press engages in lying, sneaking, prying, gossiping, and tattling, just as our very worst and very noseiest next-door neighbor might do. The press degrades its own dignity when it stoops to such levels. As for the public contaminated by such practices, their appetite for scandal and misinformation and spurious attacks on the government grows in direct proportion to the amount of garbage fed them.

"Watergate made the press a knight in shining armor. And Watergate, admittedly, was one of the press's finest hours, resulting in the very necessary tumbling of a corrupt president. But the press has become exceedingly corrupt and puffed up with its own importance ever since.

"To deliberately reveal this nation's espionage activities, to expose agents in the field to danger and even death from our enemies, to place in the hands of an ignorant, hostile, and apathetic public the debate of how this country's covert foreign policy ought to be conducted is not only an act of the gravest irresponsibility, it is an act of treason, and ought to be treated as such."

Sitting in a chair close to the Old Man, Justin could feel a sense of general discontent among the listeners at the Old Man's blanket indictment of the American press. And while the analysis was impassioned and necessarily one-sided—the Old Man Spoke as the head of a U.S. intelligence facility that was constantly being attacked by the press, and often found itself fighting Americans with one hand and the enemy with the other—Justin was convinced that the Old Man was right.

A general sense of permissiveness had made intelligence personnel and counterespionage agents the favorite targets of the very people that they were defending from outside subversion. Liberal-minded Americans seemed unaware that their liberties were often bought with the blood of others. Just as the American prosperity depended in large part on outside exploitation. The principal error, Justin thought, was in contrasting and even opposing systems of capitalism functioning under other names.

Still, the U.S. intelligence system was under fire at home and abroad. Much of this, Justin thought, was due to the not-so-recent discovery of spies by novelists, motion pictures, and the press. Spies were now seen as cold-blooded, heartless monsters rather than as patriotic human beings who willingly put their lives on the line for the sake of their country. And the misunderstanding and sometimes even the willful arrogance of an uninformed public made every act by loyal agents a cause for vilification and outcry.

"The system that I have devised for the men under my immediate command," the Old Man said, "is complex and very simple at the same time. First of all, I plan to appear to go along with our critics. We shall appear to be open, moralistic, and responsive to public criticism, and lend ourselves to the voices of defeat."

Murmurs of protest went up from the room. The Old Man waited until they died down. "Gentlemen, we are concerned with the preservation of freedom. Of course, the communists say the exact same thing. Except that we must believe that we are the very opposite of communism, or we shall indeed go down to defeat. And to preserve freedom, no act is too despicable.

"We are professionals; the public, by definition, is an amateur in the matter of deceit. And deceit is what we are all about, gentlemen. We must learn to give the appearance of naiveté. We must balance fact against probability and know beforehand what the outcome of the operation and the public reaction will be. Then we must tailor the end to suit our own needs, our own methods, and our own ends."

"Why, it sounds just like writing a mystery!" one voice said.

The Old Man's grin was full of pure malice. "That is exactly what it sounds like," he said. And so the Old Man's assignment sheets were born, not only as a defense against America's enemies, but as a safeguard against certain American elements as well.

The business of spying and of chasing down the nation's enemies to chop their heads off, at least in the Old Man's Special Assignments Division, could be likened to the trajectory of a vehicle almost blindly following a hazardous route.

And waiting for—indeed, even inviting, and hoping for, and sometimes even gleefully causing—a series of carefully planned accidents to happen which would be pleasing to the grumpy taxpayer and, at the same time, make the CIA appear to be a bunch of cub scouts with Dear Abby as den mother.

The late afternoon sun came through the car window on Justin's side, warming him. Justin was thinking about that historic meeting at Langley as he rode beside Joel Peters on his way to the asylum at Riverview. Could Peters be a SADIF agent after all, Justin wondered. An unexpected part of SADIF's carefully planned mystery?

No; Joel Peters was harmless, Justin decided. This "mystery" had to do with elements, concocted by SADIF and the CIA in equal portions, that were clearly beyond the round little man's reach.

A truckload of dynamite masquerading as pumpkins and driven by a beautiful girl, like something out of a mad Cinderella story. High-society people eating rats and drinking champagne at the Waldorf-Astoria—why did the Old Man think that that was so important? And insane asylums being raided simultaneously throughout all of North America by SADIF—the purpose of which was still not clear and might never be.

And now, the entrance of somebody named Andrea McKay as FLP candidate into the presidential primaries, which had just been announced on the car radio.

"Andrea McKay, of all things!" Joel Peters exclaimed happily, brought from his sulking mood by the announcement. "I know her! She's from Carlton, grew up there. Her mother is dead, but her father still lives there."

He glanced sideways at Justin, as though apologizing for having broken the silence. He drove carefully, like an old woman carrying a cargo of eggs. "The mother died several years ago under peculiar circumstances," he said. "I did the story about it. Perhaps I'll have the chance to tell you about it sometime."

"Perhaps," Justin said. "Listen, Peters, I apologize for being such a shit awhile back. But I'm nervous and tense . . . you know how it is, going to a new job, and all that. . . ."

Peters was mollified, breaking out in a big grin; his faith in mankind had been restored. "Think nothing of it! I get that way myself sometimes." He twisted behind the wheel and stuck a white calling card into Justin's jacket pocket. "Listen, once you get settled in at the sanatarium, why don't you drop over to Carlton? It's just twenty-six miles away, over the Mississippi bridge. You can have dinner with me and my mother. She's an invalid, but I'm a swell cook. We don't have much company, but I'm sure she'll like you."

So, it was a mother after all. Justin felt sorry for the poor bastard. "Thanks," he said. "I might need that, after a few days in a madhouse." He collected his briefcase, for he saw a sign ahead announcing the Riverview Sanatarium at the next turnoff.

Peters laughed. "Oh, I don't think you'll find it so bad. The sanatarium, I mean. Dr. Porter runs a very tight ship."

They drove in silence for a while until Peters pulled the car off the highway and came to a stop at a modest entrance set between massive bulks of hedgerow. Further up the short road, Justin could see large, wrought-iron gates with the name of the sanatarium bolted across them in bright bronze letters.

"Well, we're here," Peters said. "You just walk right up that road."

Justin thanked him and got out. "You've been very kind, Peters. I just might take you up on that invitation after all."

"You're welcome anytime," Peters said. "I'm pretty proud of my Chinese cooking. Mother likes it too." He smiled and waved. Then he backed the car out, turned it around, and drove off down the highway.

Looking at the somber, brooding facade of the Riverview facility as he approached it down the short, gravel road, Justin hoped that he would not have to stay in the place for an entire month. But, as it developed, he would stay for much longer.

He would remember later that he had not been altogether comfortable after the large iron gates were opened by a surly guard to his ring, and then he was led across a brown lawn and past some trees up a walkway into a gingerbread-looking old Victorian mansion, into the offices of Dr. Steve Porter, director of the Riverview Sanatarium.

Dr. Porter was a big, embarrassed-looking bear of a man with a seedy complexion and a full head of shaggy brown hair. His office, like the rest of the house that seemed to make up the administrative section, had obviously been renovated at great expense. "Welcome to Riverview, Dr. Weston," Porter said amiably. "We were told to expect you. And I can see that you will be a welcome addition to the staff, for we have many female patients here. It's good for their therapy to have an attractive young doctor around. Most of our professionals nowadays turn their backs on this kind of work for private practice, which is more lucrative, I'd dare say."

"Yes, I'd say so," Justin ventured. Porter's handshake

was somewhat limp and damp, as though he'd offered Justin a used handkerchief. He suggested a drink—there was a small bar in one corner of the spacious room, comfortable leather chairs, reproductions of the Mona Lisa and Venus rising from the sea foam. Justin decided on a whiskey; Porter made two, with a dash of soda, and took a gulp from his as he limped across the red velvet carpeting to hand Justin his.

"An old war wound," he said, thumping his index finger against his left leg. "A bomb took it off in Korea."

"Sorry," Justin murmured. The man's eyes were small, brown, and piercing, his gaze a kind of rapier reaching out and flicking Justin with open sharpness.

"Were you in the war, Dr. Weston?"

"In Vietnam." He moved over to the window where red drapes hung on each side of the broad, polished glass. The room, with its carpet, its paintings, and its bar, made him think of an old-fashioned whorehouse. He had the sensation that he ought to ask Dr. Porter where the madame was.

"Yes, Vietnam. Well, I'd say you chaps had a rougher time of it than we did. Although all war is hell, wouldn't you say?"

"I'd say so." He felt that the man was stalling for time, and wondered why. Perhaps there was a madame in the picture after all.

"Well, yes. Yes, I'd say you're right. At any rate, I suppose you know about your salary, and tenure, things like that." At Justin's nod, he went on. "Riverview is a small, exclusive sanatarium, as you might know. We have some very important people here as patients. Some of them are quite beyond the pale. Others are no more than drunk cases, confined here for a drying-out period. But we do our utmost to maintain the very highest professional standards, no matter what the illness might be."

"I understand that," Justin said. God, the guy was a bore! British, or something. Maybe even Canadian. Despite his spotless white smock, Justin had the impression that Dr. Porter was about as much of a "doctor" as he himself was.

He could judge from the window that Dr. Porter's offices were on the top floor of three others, and the river view of the sanatarium's name apparently had to do with a kind of small, muddy tributary from the Mississippi, a thin pink snake that crawled through a distant meadow on the far side of the highway. He could also see modern brick buildings fanning out from the old-fashioned mansion in the form of a quadrangle around a garden that had given in to the ravages of fall. Considering the size of the place, he was impressed by the small number of people he could see. He turned away from the window and found Dr. Porter's eyes studying him intently.

He seemed embarrassed and gulped from his drink. "Well, Dr. Weston, it really *is* a pleasure to have you here with us. You may find that we do things in a somewhat unorthodox way here. But we have found our methods to be quite effective. Among other things, we encourage our female patients to give full vent to their fantasies, rather than repressing them, which is the usual approach to therapy. Most of our patients here, I might add, are women who have known the violence of passion."

Justin nodded. "A rather poetic way of putting it," he said.

Dr. Porter seemed to be pleased at the comment. "Yes . . . yes . . . Well, we're doing some pretty revolutionary things here in correcting sexual dysfunctions, if I do say so myself. Our male psychiatrists deal with sex therapy personally, and in the most meaningful way possible."

"You mean fucking?" Justin said bluntly.

"Well, if you want to put it that way," Dr. Porter said

primly. He was very red in the face, and limped rapidly to the bar. "You mean, you didn't know?" He gulped a large whiskey, straight.

"I didn't know," Justin said truthfully. Another little detail the Old Man hadn't bothered to mention in his assignment sheets, Justin thought.

Dr. Porter's redness had abated some; he seemed fortified now, and very much the drunk. "Well, now that that's settled, Dr. Weston . . . I wonder if you'd mind awfully taking off your clothes?"

"Not at all," Justin answered in the same tone of reasonableness. He was convinced now that Dr. Porter, if he was a doctor, was as nutty as a fruitcake.

He stripped naked for Porter's benefit. Again the man's face went beet red as he perused Justin. "Yes, yes . . .you'll do quite well, Dr. Weston. Our women will certainly be pleased. You may get dressed now. Yes, that's it. Then someone will escort you to your quarters. And you'll be shown around the establishment. To get your bearings, so to speak. But please understand that I am always available to listen to your views, your suggestions, your complaints, any little thing that might come up. . . ."

But Justin was thinking about fucking a bunch of demented old women as he left Dr. Porter's office, conducted by a fairly good-looking nurse in white uniform that showed off her broad ass. Well, it might not be all that bad, he thought, if the women weren't *too* much off their rocker and if they weren't too old. As for Riverview Sanatarium, he thought he might understand why SADIF had overlooked this place when they'd raided madhouses a few days ago. It was probably too crazy for them. If he'd been a real doctor, he'd be on his way to Chicago by now. Riverview Sanatarium didn't want a psychiatrist; they wanted a fucking stud!

Later on, in his quarters, which faced west, he watched

the sun preparing to go down—amassing a spectrum of colors around itself like a woman putting on gaudy makeup—while he was telephoning to a Chicago safe number for more clothing to be sent to him. From the way things looked out here in the boondocks, they'd probably only have overalls for sale. Although Joel Peters and Dr. Porter both had been well dressed.

Thinking of Dr. Porter again, Justin wondered what the old boy's game really was. He and Joel Peters had both been singularly unobservant in not asking Justin about his luggage, although that could have been either politeness or just a plain oversight. Still, looking back, there had been several things about the encounter with Joel Peters, the editor from Carlton, that nagged at him now.

Why had Peters been on the highway in the first place? And why had the highway been so conveniently deserted just at the time the abortive ambush took place? And was it important that Joel Peters said he knew Andrea McKay, the newly declared presidential candidate for the Federalist-Liberal party? The SADIF party? Could Joel Peters be SADIF after all?

His imagination seemed to be running away with him, and he forced himself to stop thinking along those lines. Instead, he wandered around the comfortable three-room apartment in the personnel area that the hospital had provided him and found it more than adequate. He was lying on the bed after showering, with a towel wrapped around his lean waist, when a knock sounded at the door.

"Come in," Justin said.

The door opened slightly, then all the way. Then, Thelma Carew—from Orlando, Florida, some twenty years ago—stepped into the room.

"Thelma!" He didn't know if that was the coolest thing to say or not—maybe she was using another name, like he was—but his surprise had been too great for control.

When he called her name, she peered at him in surprise, apparently not recognizing him. Not at first. Then she gave a short cry and called him by that other name which he had given up on joining the Death Squad.

"Roger! Roger Johnson! My God! What on earth are *you* doing here?"

He pressed his finger to her lips, then swept her into his arms, liking the way her slender boy melted against his, then pulled away.

"Call me Dr. Weston," he whispered into her ear. "The room might be bugged." Although he'd looked for listening devices, there was still the possibility that he'd missed one.

Her large brown eyes grew even wider, but he saw that she understood at once. "Oh . . . I'm afraid I've made a terrible mistake. Do forgive me, Dr. Weston. I thought you were an old childhood friend. But he was killed in the war."

She stretched out her hand very professionally; he thought that she was beautiful in her white smock, her flaming red hair stylishly bobbed, the full lips he'd remembered from that summer so long ago.

"I am Dr. Thelma Carew," she said, quite formally. "Dr. Porter, the director, asked me to show you around the hospital and to get you settled in."

If she noticed the sudden erection he carried underneath the towel—he was thinking about all the times he'd possessed that yielding body—her professional manner did not change in the least. Also, it would take a pretty clever listening device to tell when a guy got a hard-on.

"That was very thoughtful of Dr. Porter," he said. "And very good of you to help me. If you'd give me a few minutes to dress . . .?"

"Of course," Thelma said. "I'll just step out into the hallway." He caught the flash of a good-looking leg as she smiled, turned, and went out the door.

So . . . Thelma Carew had come back quite unexpectedly into his life, Justin mused as he changed into hospital whites that he'd got from the emergency room. He'd told them that his own baggage had been held up at the airport, and that he'd come on without it.

Again he was struck by the fact that no one seemed to think it strange that he should arrive only with a briefcase, like some kind of a businessman. Did they know about the explosion, that his car and clothing had been totally destroyed? Either that, or they had extremely lousy security, in a place where security ought to be at its very best. For all they knew, if they really were on the level, he might just be any bum coming in on them from the highway.

Or they might be SADIF agents, although Dr. Porter's photograph wasn't in the Old Man's assignment sheet either. But that was not unusual; the Old Man couldn't possibly know about every SADIF operative that Justin would come across as he tried to unravel this puzzle. Had he stumbled into a SADIF nest? If so, they knew about the explosion; and somebody would probably make another attempt on his life before too long.

He'd considered the possibility since he'd first stepped through the main gate. Porter impressed him as being as phony as a three-dollar bill. And on Justin's way here to his quarters, he'd glimpsed only a few people here and there, all of whom seemed to belong to staff. So far, except perhaps for Dr. Porter himself, Justin hadn't seen a single indication that mental patients were present in this building. Riverview Sanatarium seemed to be a very strange place indeed.

And stranger still that Thelma Carew should be here at Riverview some twenty years since he'd last seen her that splendid summer in Orlando. Dr. Thelma Carew, she'd said. He remembered that she'd known expressions like *mother fixation* and words like *scatological*, and that she'd said she wanted to be a doctor, although he'd clearly disbelieved her at the time.

Well, she'd apparently been very serious. And she looked absolutely great in her doctor's outfit. But what was she really doing here at Riverview? There was no mention of her either in the assignment sheets, but Justin was far too pragmatic to accept Thelma's being here as one of those pleasant coincidences. But whatever the reason, he was glad as hell to see her again. Although he noticed that she had fallen into the caution game with almost practiced ease when he'd told her about the possibility of the room being bugged.

My God! he wondered. Was everybody a spy or a secret agent nowadays? No wonder the press went ape shit about the least little thing that had to do with the CIA. America apparently had spies coming out of its ears, like Lisbon during World War II. Dessed now in hospital whites that fitted him rather well, he went out into the hallway where Thelma Carew awaited him.

"Now you look more professional," she said with a smile. But she squeezed his hand with the same intimacy he remembered from so long ago. And he rewarded her with a warm grin. He wondered if she knew his dick was still hard; she had that effect on him.

"I'm glad you like the uniform, Dr. Carew. Shall we get started on our tour?"

"We shall," she said. She turned and started down the corridor. She was tall, slender, and very sexy, despite her hospital whites. The faint fragrance of her exotic perfume haunted Justin's nostrils like sweet ghosts.

He had been mistaken in supposing that Riverview Sanatarium—"We all call it Riverview Hospital," Thelma said; "sanatarium sounds like something to do with garbage trucks"—was less than it ought to be. Being Friday evening, Thelma explained, staff was reduced to a minimum;

also, many patients who were well enough to do so left Friday afternoon to spend the weekend with responsible families or friends.

Riverview Hospital was enormous, modern, well equipped, and very impressive. There were several buildings with open wards, dozens of private rooms, the usual hospital health and clinical services, and a modern operating room on the top level of the four-story building that constituted the medical center.

In a spacious area adjoining the hospital buildings, there were separate cottages and even houses with private staffs for patients who could afford it. There were also recreational areas, with everything from swimming pools to tennis courts, bowling alleys, hobby rooms, a modest motion picture theater, a golf course, riding stable, helicopter pad, interfaith chapels, and, finally, the caged-in isolation area where Riverview's most disturbed patients were kept under lock and key.

"There are more than fifteen hundred patients at Riverview," Thelma said, "with about 120 or so considered to be of the dangerous variety. Most of the patients, however, have what could be called normal personality or psychological dislocations. As for staff, we number 217 at peak level. Although, as I have said, you can see that we are operating now on a weekend schedule."

"Very impressive," Justin said. "And what's your role in all of this, Dr. Carew?" Absorbed by the tour, he'd found it easy to maintain the myth that he and Thelma were strangers to each other. "I'm in clinical psychiatry myself."

Her lovely brown eyes filled with amusement; it was clear that she didn't believe him. "I am chief of hospital services," she said. "Clinical psychiatry also happens to be my own field as well."

Justin nodded. He was indeed impressed by what he'd

seen of Riverview; and he'd enjoyed being with Thelma. And he wondered what on earth it was that the Old Man thought could be diabolical about a place like Riverview.

As for Thelma, she'd been brisk and efficient as a tour guide and had never alluded to that eventful summer in Orlando, not even when they were clearly in areas where their voices could not possibly be monitored.

But Justin had been aware of every painful minute that he was with her that he wanted Thelma just as badly as he'd wanted her in the old days. His loins absolutely ached for her as they walked across the quadrangle in the glare of spotlights holding back the outer darkness.

"Well, it's dinnertime now," Thelma said, checking her wristwatch. "Would you like to get something in the dining room? Then there's a motion picture afterwards in the theater. The show begins at eight o'clock. I understand that it's a spy picture."

Were her eyes trying to tell him something? The years had filled her out, both above and below, from what he could tell through that damnable smock. But her eyes were as expressive as ever; had he seen a warning in them? A hint of fear?

"I'm starving," he said, rubbing his flat belly. "And the movie would be nice, provided they have popcorn." At least his hunger was no lie. He'd had nothing all day except for the sandwiches from the airport. And the last one of them had been blown up by the dynamited pumpkins. "To coin a bright new phrase," he said, smiling, "I'm hungry enough to eat a horse."

Thelma laughed musically. "And you probably will, if some of the complaints we hear about the food are true. Let's go find out. The dining hall is down this way."

Horse or not, the food was excellent. He put away two large baked pork chops, a double helping of mashed potatoes and spinach, two slices of apple pie, and three cups of strong, bitter coffee. Thelma had a small salad and talked about inconsequential things as Justin gulped down his food like a caveman.

"God, I was starved!" he said, wiping his mouth with a napkin.

"I like to see a man eat," Thelma said. And then their eyes locked; it was no longer possible to keep the old days out. For she'd used that same expression as she'd sat across the table from him at Aunt Eugenia's, watching him wolf down his breakfast: "I like to see a man eat," she'd said. "It builds up his sperm."

The spacious dining hall had about a dozen other people scattered around, none of them very close to Thelma and Justin. He leaned closer to her, keeping his voice low. "Can we talk now, Thelma?"

She was smoking a cigarette; she gave him one and held her lighter to it. What was it he saw in her eyes? The gold flecks put there by the lights gave him the impression of whirling like atoms around a nucleus.

"I am certainly pleased that you were impressed by Riverview, Dr. Weston. It was a pleasure to show you around."

Like hell they could talk! Warning bells went off inside his head as she stood up, straightening out her smock. The Colt .38 was suddenly cold against his belly where he had it jammed down inside his waistband.

"I must go now and see a few patients," she said. Her smile was strained, completely false. And her eyes were definitely full of fear. "I'm sure we'll be seeing each other again, Dr. Weston. Perhaps in the movie." Before he could say anything, she was gone, her high heels clicking with a hollow sound on the cement floor.

He paid the bill and went to his apartment with a sense of great unease. Thelma's surprising response to him in the dining hall had unsettled him. She had directly sidestepped his question about it being safe to talk, and had even called him *Dr. Weston* with greater emphasis.

She knew fucking well who he was. So something was very definitely wrong here at Riverview, and Thelma had perhaps risked her life trying to tell him so. *I understand that the picture is about spies*, she'd said, before they went into dinner. And then she'd said that *perhaps* they'd be seeing each other in the movie. Had she been telling him that they could talk safely there?

Once inside his apartment, he double-locked the door behind him. A great lot of good that would do, he thought, if anybody really wanted to get in through the paneled wooden door. Then he sat himself down for the next half hour, studying every detail of the assignment sheets until the details there were committed to memory.

Then he burned the sheets in the metal wastebasket and flushed the ashes down the toilet. He opened the window and fanned the smoke out, feeling like a little boy trying to hide the evidence of his cigarette. Then he did the same thing with the photographs, studying every detail of the known or suspected SADIF agents' faces before burning them.

The photographs flamed up at once, although the ashes were more difficult to flush. But he finally did so, then washed out the wastebasket in the tub. Then washed the tub out. Again the nursery rhyme came to mind: the rat eats the cheese, the cat eats the rat. . . .

And who would come to devour him? He knew that he was in immense danger, that something was going to happen very soon. His body was filled with a sharp sense of menace and expectation, the climate of his system responding to the imminence of danger in the same way that tension and a heavy quiet settle over the countryside before a summer storm.

Closing the window, he went back to his briefcase. He

broke out the two extra weapons there—his .38 Special was still jammed down inside of his belt. There was a Magnum .57 with steel-jacketed bullets that could blast a hole in a man as big around as a bucket. And a snub-nosed, blue steel .38 Smith & Wesson revolver, which he sometimes liked to use alternately with the Colt Special of the same caliber.

Using adhesive from a spool in the briefcase, he taped the Magnum to the underside of the porcelain covering over the water box in the toilet. But it was when he was placing the Smith & Wesson that the small hairs on the back of his neck rose like an angry dog's.

He had found the bug. It was installed in the very back of the drawer in the bedside stand.

He felt a glow of certainty now that Riverview was a SADIF nest. Nothing up to this point had actually confirmed it. Dr. Porter might easily have been just an amiable nut. And Thelma could have been playing some kind of game. It wouldn't be the first time she'd toyed with him, he thought, remembering the so-called sacrifice with the girl named Betty on the hood of the Model-T Ford.

But finding the bug convinced him that a hell of a lot more was going on here at Riverview than met the eye. The listening device was of a new, highly sophisticated type. The "screaming bugs," they were called. Hardly larger than a scarab, attached to cobweb-thin wire, they were designed to scream their heads off if you touched them or tried to disable them. That way, the listener would know that the device had been found.

Justin had taken out the drawer to tape the Smith & Wesson to its underside when he saw the device. To a less knowledgeable observer, it might have been merely the remnants of a rather large bug. The hairy perimeter of extremely fine wires would pick up sound and transmit it to powerful receivers where SADIF agents were listening, probably as close as in the next room. Although he doubted that; the device had an extremely long range.

So, they'd heard his telephone call to Chicago asking for more clothing. And they'd heard Justin and Thelma's surprised exchange when she'd entered the room. Had the bug also picked up his whispered warning to her? Working quickly and carefully, he taped the Smith & Wesson to the bottom of the drawer, as he'd originally planned. They would hardly expect him to do that. Although stashing away the guns was only a precautionary measure; any trained searcher intent on finding them would be onto them in fifteen or twenty minutes.

As for the rest of the paraphernalia in his briefcase, it seemed normal enough. An electric razor, a completely innocent and gimmic-free copy of a novel by a writer named Hal Bennett, a toothbrush, and a tube of fluoride paste.

As for his wallet with the phony cards identifying him as Dr. George Weston, well, he guessed he was stuck with that. He slid the Colt .38 on the carpet beneath the bed, just far enough inside so that he could still reach and get it if necessary. He had a feeling that it was going to be necessary.

Then he stretched out on the bed and waited. His heart was pounding with anticipation as he smoked a cigarette. Whatever was going to happen would happen soon now. He heard clock bells from somewhere clang out the hour of eight. Thelma might be waiting for him in the movie.

Well, she'd have to wait. If she was SADIF, he'd probably be walking into some kind of trap there. And if she was on his side, the best thing he could do to help her was to stay as far away from her as he could. In any event, if he was going to be attacked, better that it happen here in his room, where at least he had the limited advantage of limited familiarity.

His cock was hard from the excitement of expectation. That frequently happened when he was like this, the tension becoming highly sexual. He rubbed his hands over it as though calming an impatient beast, and self-love welled up in him like a bubbling spring, stifling anxiety.

Was this how it would all end? he thought. Would he be locked up in a madhouse for the rest of his life? It was like his most hideous fear come true. He knew that SADIF had ways to make him completely disappear, so effectively that even the Old Man, with all his cleverness, could never find him. A horrible thing to contemplate, Justin thought; he'd rather be dead than condemned to that kind of madness.

Then, he heard the faraway clock strike the quarter hour. At the same time, a soft knock sounded on the door. They had finally come.

THREE

Four months later, a mere shadow of the man who had called himself Justin Perry sat on the floor of a padded cell in the dangerous inmates' section of Riverview Sanatarium, his back to the wall, his knees drawn up against his chest.

Terrible, unspeakable things had happened to Justin Perry in the last four months. And while his mind remained strong and clear most of the time, there were frightening moments when he feared that he would go off the edge altogether.

He was watched over day and night by guards. His food was pushed through a round sort of large rat hole to him on a pink plastic tray bolted down on a pink plastic trolley. He ate the food off the tray rapidly—with his bare hands; no utensils of any kind were provided—before it was snatched back from him on the trolley.

Water, milk, and other liquids came in molded receptacles that formed part of the tray. He had to kneel down and suck up the liquids through plastic straws, then he had to turn the straws over to the guards, under threat of severe punishment. Although he had not yet tried suicide, every precaution had been taken against it.

In his more lucid moments, he was aware that none of this had been mentioned in the Old Man's assignment sheet, certainly nothing about Justin's being locked away in a madhouse. So much for trying to track down the enemy with a movie script, he sometimes thought bitterly. At any rate, he was completely on his own; whatever may or may not have been on the assignment sheet was forgotten in his agony, the faces on the destroyed photographs an indistinguishable blur. His dreams were filled with slime and gore, as though his mind had turned to muck. Frequently, he woke up during the night in a cold sweat.

In the beginning, he had been full of fight and rebelliousness, destroying the food on the tray rather than eating it, relieving himself on the padded floor or up against the matted walls rather than in the plastic gadgets that were brought to him three times a day to receive his waste. He was frightened, and tried to hide it in anger and defiance.

But they simply stopped giving him nourishment; he was left to rot in his own excrement. Until some mechanism in his head clicked—the will to survive slyly asserting itself—and he realized that conformity, or at least the appearance of conformity, was probably the only insurance that he might some day walk out of Riverview alive.

Alive! What a sweet-sounding word! He, an assassin, had never really known the true importance of being alive until it appeared that he was at death's door. And not threatened in those heroic four or five minutes, or even four or five hours, or four or five days, that usually make up the mandatory menace to the hero before the altogether predictable resolution.

No, not that kind of temporary menace. Riverview had taught him that there were menaces, tortures, and fears that conceivably could go on forever, given the skill with which they were applied and the physical and emotional conditions of the person being menaced, and tortured, and terrified.

Justin had been in excellent physical condition when he'd awakened naked four months ago in this cell. It was the psychological part that threatened to betray him. If he had formerly feared madness because the woman he'd thought was his mother had appeared mad, now he was certain that the unknown woman who'd given birth to and then abandoned him was far madder than the one who'd become her substitute.

It was not a moral judgment about the unknown mother; in those moments when he felt himself to be insane, it was as though the vehicle of his mind had simply switched over to another track that he had not even suspected existed. When he felt madder than the woman that his father had killed, he placed the blame on the woman his father impregnated, and felt that his insanity dangled like a Christmas bauble from the umbilical cord of a merry accumulation of madness handed down to him by the unknown mother.

He felt like throwing his head back and screaming. His body began trembling uncontrollably. He felt like a large child in an even larger womb, without the hope of rebirth. And with the loss of hope, the real horrors set in. He found himself swinging from the idealistic stance of trying to focus on the problems of the world—was there still a world? If so, he was almost completely cut off from it inside of this grotesque and gray-shadowed womb, never even allowed outside for exercise or sun, if there still was a sun—back into an institutionalized selfishness inside of which he felt mean, ugly, completely alone.

That he *was* alone seemed less important than his sense that people no longer counted in his life, nor he in theirs, that the struggle upward didn't matter anymore, that salvation and success and all the other noble labels were merely that—labels painted on people. But those were the times when he was thinking clearly. There were other times when his mind resembled mush.

He could not think, as though he floundered around inside of tepid oatmeal. Indeed, he could barely talk or control his arms or legs. He polluted himself without knowing or meaning to. They took away his clothes and left him with a smelly blanket to cover himself with until the crisis had passed. What caused those attacks? He didn't know, but he suspected they were putting something in his food. But why? Hadn't they found out everything they wanted to know with their injections and their infernal machines?

For the first time in his adult life, he actually feared for his manhood, that he would be raped by another man. In the beginning, the guards amused themselves by sticking their erect penises through the bars in lewd invitation. But the worst sort of penetration that they did to him physically had to do with his nostrils.

They shook up bottles of club soda, building the pressure in the bottles by corking it with a finger. Then they popped the finger out after the soda was boiling and held Justin's head while the volcanic mixture shot up his nose. He would have screamed if he could have, but the boiling soda filled his nose and ran down into his mouth and throat, gagging him. That was in the very beginning, when men who said they were police came to ask him questions.

"Why did you blow up the truck and the tollbooth on the highway?" they asked. "Once you have been psychiatrically evaluated, you will stand trial for murder."

"What terrorist group are you working with? Where is their headquarters? Why do you call yourself Dr. George Weston when your real name is Michel Dupré? We have checked your fingerprints with the FBI in Washington."

So, at least the fingerprint apparatus was still working;

his real fingerprints in Washington were indeed identified as belonging to Michel Dupré, a French terrorist. Justin received some satisfaction from that.

"We know that you were involved in the explosion at the tollbooth," they went on. "You are guilty of three murders there. Your footprints were found in the damp earth; casts of them match your own shoes. What terrorist group? Who is your boss? Where are your headquarters?"

"We have picked up your contact in Chicago, and we have a tape of the coded telephone call you made, supposedly asking for clothing. But a suitcase arrived here at the sanatarium under your phony name of Dr. George Weston. It contained dynamite, caps, timing devices. What terrorist group do you work with?"

Heavy-jawed men with brutal muscles, they shot club soda up his nose, administered electric shocks to his genitals, beat him professionally with hard fists to the belly and the kidneys to leave him unmarked. He urinated blood for several days afterwards.

"You've got it all wrong," he heard himself mutter. "I'm Dr. George Weston. I'm a psychiatrist. I'm not a terrorist. Calls this telephone number in Washington—they'll set you straight. . . ."

He said the safe number at Langley so many times that it remained etched on his brain, even when they shot him full of drugs and attached him to machines to monitor the truth of what he said. He had a fine contempt for machines, and apparently fooled them.

Then the men came back and began the questioning all over again. "What terrorist group are you with? Why did you blow up the truck and the tollbooth? We know you were there . . . your footprints . . . the rented Ford from Avis. . . ."

Their steel fists beat him brutally, but very carefully. Were they really going to take him to court? He felt lost inside a surrealistic painting done by Dali in one of the Spaniard's darker moods.

"Call the number. . . . I am Dr. George Weston, psychiatrist. . . ." It was the CIA's safe number in Langley. They would either back his history or tell the cops to leave him the hell alone, that he was on a national defense assignment.

Then Thelma came to see him one day. He knew what he must have looked and smelled like—he absolutely stank; they never let him bathe for weeks after they'd thrown him into the cell. His beard had grown out like matted black wire; his hair fell down into his face and around his shoulders. He must have looked like a wild beast; he certainly felt like one.

"Thelma. . . ." Was she going to get him out of here? Would she say it was all a mistake? "I didn't do any of those things they say. Get me out of here, Thelma. Call this number in Virginia." He told her the number; it seemed that she wrote it down. "They think I'm crazy," he said, unable to hide the fear.

She looked at him searchingly. "But you did get naked in Dr. Porter's office, didn't you?" She showed him a photo; he was standing there with his long dick hanging down. They must have had a hidden camera.

That rocked him. "Dr. Porter asked me to get naked, damn it! He said that the male psychiatrists here fucked the women patients."

Her eyes darkened; she clearly disbelieved him. "Dr. Porter would never say something like that, Dr. Weston. He is a very serious professional."

Dr. Weston. She'd called him *Dr. Weston*! She was probably the only person here who knew who he really was, and yet she'd called him by that phony name. Why? Did they send her here to get something out of him that they couldn't?

God, he wanted to fuck. Beaten, battered, covered with filth, naked underneath the dirty blanket, nothing to eat but bread and water for so long he couldn't even remember . . . and he wanted to fuck.

"Thelma . . ." He reached out to her with a hairy, clawlike hand; his nails had grown very long. "Thelma, I need you. . . ." He pulled the blanket back weakly, showing her.

She stood abruptly, and fled, her eyes full of terror. And of something else too. She wouldn't fuck him, but she had insisted on calling him Dr. Weston. *Not* Roger Johnson, which was his real name, the name he'd used when he'd known her in Orlando, the name he'd given up when he'd joined the CIA, convinced that the safety of the people is the highest law. Justin Perry, assassin. Shit. Not a single one of them had called him Justin Perry.

There was something almost Siberian about his isolation. Like being back in the time of the Czars, reading Dostoevski or one of the other gloomy Russians by candlelight in the middle of a snowstorm on the frozen steep steppes; stark naked in a metal chair; both feet jammed into a bucket of icy water; Tschaikovsky's *Pathétique* symphony playing desolately in the background.

And then, the men again. "As a favor to the lady doctor, we called that telephone number you gave us. Good thing we did. They never heard of you, bigshot. So, who're you working for? You might as well talk, buddy. But we've got time, since you're going to be here for a long time. You've been officially committed. You're too crazy to stand trial, the doctors say. Even the lady doctor says that."

His mouth turned dry; his whole body went cold. "How do you mean, crazy? And who committed me? You know fucking well I'm not crazy!" He fought to keep from trembling. *"Who the fuck committed me?"*

They could see his naked fear—he couldn't help it now; it had to show after all these months—and grinned at it. "How do we know? But we got the papers here." Holding them up, snatching them away elaborately when he tried to reach for them. "The name's here: Donald Sandburg, it says. Some federal judge okayed it. You're *committed*, buddy. No doubt about it."

It seemed impossible that any human power would ever bring him back to hope again. But they had called Langley as a favor to Thelma. Although she had also agreed that he was mad enough to be locked away.

Officially committed. The order signed by Donald Sandburg and some federal judge. *Donald Sandburg was the Old Man's name.* Why would the Old Man have him committed? And why hadn't somebody from the CIA come to get him out of this place?

He didn't know the answers, but at least the Old Man knew where he was, had even signed documents committing him. He leaned his head back against the wall and tried to think of pleasant things. And his mind went back to that night four months ago when he'd heard the light knock on the door and had gone to open it.

He'd been hoping that it was Thelma, coming up with some explanations. But it was five strange women instead. All of them extraordinarily beautiful, they were dressed in filmy gowns with nothing on underneath. They brought fruit and wine, stepping into the room with a friendly familiarity, helping him out of his clothes as they giggled like Japanese geishas.

The orgy went on for hours. He was too pleased and surprised to ask questions, and then he was too busy to think about the strangeness of it. He was a man who more often than not allowed himself to be led by his peter, and this time he was really led well. There were two blondes and three brunettes. They told him their names during the course of that evening, but he got to know them better through the taste and texture of their vaginas, the flavor of their lips, the shape and substance of their breasts, even the differing gasps and moans they made as he ground down inside them like a hungry corkscrew.

Of course he knew that he was in danger. But he thought that there was little possibility of the women killing him with their pussies. And they had brought nothing other than their luscious bodies, and the too-sweet wine and the not so ripe fruit, which they nibbled at while waiting their turn to nibble at him. He had not forgotten the listening device in the drawer next to the bed. Apparently, neither had they; most of that evening was filled with giggles and groans, the thud of bodies and the slopping sounds of cunts and mouths, as the evening wore on into night and the women unsuccessfully tried to wear him down. But he was more than a match for them, and during a period of rest before the next onslaught, he found himself thinking of the first woman that he had ever killed.

She was an exotic Albanian operative who'd killed six U.S. intelligence agents. Her total kill was said to number more than a dozen male and female agents. She made forays into the Western intelligence apparatus and made off with lives and top-secret documents with the impunity of a wolf raiding a henhouse.

She was called Big Bertha by the CIA. Varying descriptions were given of her, but none was considered accurate. Big Bertha was a clever killer, coming and going like a shadow. She was said to be a master of disguises; her trademark was the way she killed her victims with a sharp metal needle inserted at the base of the skull into the brain. Obviously a man hater, she mutilated male agents, generally slashing off their penises and taking them with her.

The Old Man assigned Justin to the case. "How am I

supposed to find her?'' Justin asked. He cringed at the idea of his peter winding up in a pickle jar.

"She'll find you," the Old Man said. "We've let it leak out that you're carrying top-secret documents to the French government. Most of Big Bertha's kills were agents picked up in Paris, that much we do know. So there's apparently a connection there somewhere. We've got to get her, Justin. And watch out for your prick."

Justin had flown into Paris on the Concorde flight from Washington. Paris was enchanting as usual, especially at the tail end of spring before the stifling summer set in. After several false contacts, Justin was soon aware that he was in the presence of Big Bertha.

She had begun the flirtation on the Champs Élysées. With silky, honey-blond hair and baby-blue eyes, she looked like everybody's eighteen-year-old girl from next door. *Petite* was the French word that described her. She had firm breasts, long slender legs, a nice ass, and a luscious red mouth that was instantly inviting.

She fluttered her blue eyes when Justin invited her to have a coffee or a drink. They crossed the famous avenue holding hands like long-time lovers. He liked the way she fell immediately into intimacy; they might have been old friends instead of two undercover agents maneuvering to annihilate each other. Except for a familiar warning quivering in his gut, Justin would have thought it impossible for her to be a killer.

She chattered on between sips from her bitter vermouth. Her eyes flashed at him like hypnotic neon signs. She made her bosom heave in a very exciting way. From time to time, her pink tongue flicked out and moved around her lips like the blade of a windshield wiper, obviously a promise of things to come. He spread his legs underneath the table to accommodate the erection there.

"You do not like your drink?" she asked. Her French was like dusky music.

"I'm too enchanted by you," he said.

Her eyes zapped him like a blue laser, then lowered. "Silly," she said. She had drifted into this place too naturally; it was not impossible that she was in league with some employee here, who might drop a drug into his drink.

She reached across the table with her milk-white arms, scooped up the drink, and gulped it down. "I do so love vermouth," she said. "Would you like to make love to me?" Her beauty, coupled with her pixie manner, was completely disarming.

"I'd love to make love to you," Justin said. "Shall we go to your place, or mine?"

"I have my car," she said. She jumped up, straightening her blue skirt. She wore a pale yellow peasant's blouse that contrived to slip off first one shoulder, then the other. "I like to make love in my car," she said. "Although it's a Peugeot and might be a bit uncomfortable for someone as tall as you. But that will make it more *intime*." She looped her feed-bag purse over her shoulder. "Come. Let us go. And do not forget your very important briefcase."

"How do you know it's important?" Justin grinned as he dropped some francs on the table.

"All briefcases are important," she said. The setting sun falling down through the latticework and vines decorating the outdoor restaurant made her seem splotched with gold.

She drove to an isolated spot near the Seine. The river gave off a rather foul odor, as though many fish had died there. When Justin entered the girl, she doubled up against him with a slight gasp, her eyes opening wider in pleasure and pain.

"I think that you might kill me with passion," she said.

68

He smiled grimly down into her shoulder. Then, quite leisurely, he reached out and stopped her upraised arm in midair, squeezing her wrist cruelly until she dropped the murderous steel pin she was about to plunge into his brain. Her cunt around his cock held him like a marvelous vise.

"How did you know?" she said. He could feel her body collapse in defeat.

"You are so real in your act that you seem artificial," he told her. "In fact, you are so gifted that you destroy the very illusion you try to create. Instead of life, you seem a very pretty death. That's what gives you away, at least to me. Henry James wrote a story about the same thing."

It was probably a very profound and even meaningless comment to make to a woman he was about to kill, and especially with his dick still inside her. Especially that part about her being a very pretty death—*une très jolie mort*; you could get away with saying things like that in French. He would have liked to see her face before he killed her, then decided against turning the overhead light on. He was sure she would be radiant with sympathy and forgiveness, the face of a martyr.

Bullfrogs in the mud along the Seine bellowed in bass voices as he choked her to death while he shot into her. It was the closest to necrophilia that he had ever come. He had a sense of terror that he might not be able to take his dick out, but it slid from her easily.

He was thinking about that incident during the orgy with the five women in his room at Riverview Hospital. Energies restored, they had gone back to work on him again. Their pussies and lips wrapped around him like animated oysters. He was fucking with his ass high in the air when he felt the bite of a syringe in his butt.

This is it, he thought. He flopped off the woman, going for his gun. Whether or not the shot was lethal to him, he intended to kill all of the women.

Then they linked arms in a kind of chorus line, faces collapsing into madness as they kicked out first one leg, then the other. "Andrea McKay for president!" they cried. "Andrea McKay for president!"

He couldn't have been more surprised if the Virgin Mary had stepped into the room. The drug was making him numb, silly. He did remember that Andrea McKay was the woman who'd announced that she was running for president on the FLP ticket. He'd heard it just that afternoon on the radio in Joel Peters's car.

Apparently, the women had heard it too. "Andrea McKay for president!" they cried, dancing back and forth. "Throw the rats out!" Their voices seemed incredibly shrill, almost inhuman to Justin, even as he was swept by a sense of contentment and the greatest well-being.

He sent his arm down—it felt like a block of cement—to the Colt .38 on the carpet underneath the bed. "Andrea for president!" the women screamed, although their voices seemed to come to him from very far away. His fingers touched cold steel. Then he fell into darkness. . . . And woke up in the padded cell.

That had been four months ago.

He'd gone through the tortures, the interrogations, the news of his commitment, the sense of being completely abandoned. He did not know how many weeks and months of days and nights he had endured until he asked one of the guards what day it was.

January 16. He had been in this cell through Thanksgiving, Christmas, and New Year's. He had a son, nearly fourteen years old now, out there in that other world. Did little Roger know where he was? Justin hoped like hell that the boy didn't. Maybe the Agency had told the boy some acceptable story. And then again, maybe they hadn't.

Anger surged through him like the flexing of a great

muscle, and then a strange sense of hope. *He had a son!* There was something to live for after all. Slowly, systematically, he began to put himself back together. He began marking off the days by ripping out pieces of string from a torn corner of the mat.

He accumulated the strings like a treasure, taking them out and counting them at night while the guards dozed. January and February ended in this fashion. He felt a firmer grip on his sanity now. They let him bathe and shave under watchful eyes, but he did it daily now. He did stretching and isometric exercises, and felt his body restoring itself to its old condition.

He asked for, and got, extra food. They seemed pleased that he was finally responding to whatever it was they wanted him to respond to. He was put into a regular cell, given a place to bathe and fresh clothing every two or three days. Well, he didn't understand what it was all about, but he enjoyed going along with them. *He had a son out there!*

But he was immensely alert for further treachery and confusion. They gave him cigarettes and shots of whiskey. "To help you relax," they said. He had been taken off medication, and the whiskey did help. He kept on with his exercises, forcing himself to eat well, to sleep well. *Roger, my son!* And then, Thelma came for him, with two guards as escorts—to take him to recreation.

"The consensus is that you might respond very positively to this kind of therapy, Dr. Weston." Thelma's eyes were clear, innocent of guilt. Then why was she calling him Dr. Weston? Didn't she know who he was? Of course she did; she'd called him Roger in the room.

If SADIF didn't know his real name, then Thelma certainly did. So, why this Dr. Weston bullshit? She looked so beautiful and competent in her doctor's outfit that he was glad to go along with her. It was March; they had taken the blinds off the windows just a few days ago and a pale yellow sun had filtered through.

He'd felt like falling down and worshiping it. The ordeal seemed to be over, and he was still alive. Alive! He knew that he would get out of this place somehow and go home to Roger, if only for a few days. But for now, he followed the slim form of Thelma down innumerable corridors until finally they came to a door marked OCCUPATIONAL THERAPY and Thelma pushed her way through, followed by Justin and the guards.

Oh shit! he thought. Now they're going to teach me to make baskets! It was a fairly large room, painted a soothing blue. And there were baskets and other examples of handicraft presumably made by inmates. There was also a row of clean blackboards, several tables where checkers and chess sets waited for players. There were five windows covered over with heavy mesh wire.

There was another table behind which sat the five women who had been in the orgy with Justin his first night there. Again they were barefooted and dressed in filmy gowns. But they seemed all business as Thelma whispered to Justin to take the single chair in front of the table. He sat down, feeling very apprehensive. Was this some kind of a joke? he wondered. The five women each had a notepad and pencil in front of them. Justin felt that he had been called before a board of inquiry. He looked over his shoulder and saw that Thelma had taken a seat at the chess table; the burly guards had taken up their positions at the door.

The woman in the middle seemed to be the presiding officer. "You have been brought here," she said, "to answer certain questions of a political nature. Whether you remain here in Riverview or not depends upon the amount of honest thought that you put into your answers. We expect your complete cooperation. If you do not cooperate with us, you will be taken back to your cell and be severely punished." She was a brunette, with eyes that were strikingly similar to Thelma's. "Is that quite clear, Dr. Weston? And do you have any questions before we begin?"

"No." He had a hundred questions. But how did you go about interrogating five madwomen with the power of punishment, if not of life and death, over your head?

"Very well," the moderator said. "Madame Secretary of State, you may put the first question."

The person so addressed was a very buxom blonde at the left end of the table. She was the only one of the five who smoked. Sending up a great billow of smoke from her cigarette, she hunched forward, resting her breasts on the table, and stabbed a finger at Justin. "How would you solve the Palestinian question?" she asked.

"The Palestinian question?" He was completely taken aback. At the same time, he heard an almost imperceptible click somewhere; someone had turned on a tape recorder. "Well," he said, matching her seriousness, scrunching forward in his chair, "I think that every people has a right to their own homeland. American policy, as I remember it, requires that the Palestinians recognize Israel as a nation; then negotiations can get under way to decide whether Arafat really speaks for the Palestinians. As I say, I am very much in favor of a Palestinian homeland, but I'm afraid that Arafat and his crew have seriously damaged their image before the public. Terrorism is not the answer to anything. To kill innocent men, women, and children in an attempt to further one's cause is to seriously damage that cause. Also, it is necessary for both the Israelis and the Palestinians to lay aside their stubbornness and to sit down and negotiate."

The women seemed pleased; they nodded at one another and even flashed him tentative smiles.

The woman sitting next to Madame Secretary of State raised her hand, was recognized by the moderator, and shot the next question to Justin. "I am Madame Secretary of Defense," she said. "I think you will agree, Dr. Weston, that defense is on everybody's mind nowadays. What do you think should be the American stance in regard to nuclear weapons?"

Justin frowned thoughtfully for a few moments, worrying his nether lip. "That is a difficult question, Madame Secretary of Defense. You see, what we are dealing with here is an established fact that increases itself the more we wander around trying to find answers to the problem. If I remember correctly, the existing nuclear arsenal has enough firepower to destroy the world a thousand times over. That is the irrefutable fact. Both Russia and the United States are in the wrong, I think, when they refuse to recognize this fact. Indeed, it ought to be the basis for every round of negotiations that takes place in the arms race. But as it is, both countries talk of greater and greater deterrents, more sophisticated armaments, and all that sort of nonsense, as though the fact has somehow become myth. Of course, unilateral disarmament on the part of the United States would be as unthinkable as the same thing on the part of the Russians. What is wanted, in my opinion, is greater exposure of the Russian and the American peoples to one another; there is a tremendous lack of trust on both sides; and it is these suspicions, in my opinion, that keeps the arms race on its maddening course. All nuclear weapons ought to be destroyed, a moratorium ought to be put on the manufacturing of others, and there should be a powerful watchdog committee to make sure that both nations stick to the spirit as well as to the letter of the agreement."

Madame Secretary of Defense nodded. "Very good, Dr. Weston. But how would you go about this rapprochement between the Russian and the American peoples?"

He grinned, and said the first thing that came to his head. "Fucking seems to be about as good a way as any," he said. Seeing the shock on their faces—it amused him, these five, half-naked whores appearing to be shocked at the idea of sex as the universal pacifier—he held up his hand to defend himself. "I am very serious, ladies. Was it not General Pershing who said that when people of different nations meet, they usually fight, but they always fuck? The idea is his; but I have borrowed it because I think that it is very accurate."

"Perhaps it is your wording that is at fault, Dr. Weston." It was the chairperson speaking, a clear reprimand in her voice.

He certainly didn't want any electric shocks to his balls tonight. "Perhaps you are right, Madame Chairwoman. Perhaps I should have said that we ought to love one another. That is a very fine Christian concept."

That seemed to bring them down off their high horses. Indeed, he thought he saw the flicker of a smile at the edges of Madame Chairwoman's full, red lips. She was the one who'd nearly sucked his asshole out through his dick, during the orgy.

"A fine Christian concept, indeed," she said. Then she turned slightly to the brunette at her left. "Will you please put your question, Madame Secretary of Labor?"

"Of course." He saw that Madame Secretary of Labor seemed somewhat ill at ease. Her feet were crossed, and she seemed to be pacifying her nerves by twiddling her lavender-painted toes. "As you know, Dr. Weston, there is a tremendous rate of unemployment on the international level. The tensions that exist between the two superpowers have their origin primarily in the search for markets, as well as the corresponding search for raw materials. The laborer—the workingman and the working woman—are caught squarely between the necessities of two opposing ideologies. How do you think that we can go about easing the unemployment situation on a worldwide basis?''

Suddenly, the madness of the whole thing hit him; he had entered into the fun of the matter without realizing, until just this minute, that those half-naked women *were for real*! Jesus, he didn't know a goddamned thing about unemployment! Or defense or even the Palestinian question, for that matter.

Now he felt that he had walked into a trap. The only way to extricate himself—if he *could* extricate himself—was to keep on going along with their game. He sneaked a glance over his shoulder and saw that Thelma was tense at her table, toying with the chess pieces, but her wide eyes were planted firmly on him. The guards at the door seemed like metal men, standing stiffly at attention, gazing off into nowhere.

"Before we can talk about unemployment," he said, searching his way carefully, "I think we have to talk about the population explosion first. There ought to be carefully planned programs, on the very highest level, to teach effective birth-control practices to the people. Indeed, I do not think that it would be a bad thing if we could guarantee, by scientific means, a zero-level birth rate for the next ten or twenty years. If we do this, we have effectively decreased the available supply of labor, as well as decreasing the mounting demand for goods and services. In the final analysis, Russia and the United States—and both are equally guilty, as I indicated in the nuclear arms question—are each maneuvering for markets and the corresponding raw materials for manufacturing goods because there is a very lucrative labor source and a high demand for the output of this labor. Unemployment is high on an international level, insofar as I see it, because high-powered technology has come into the picture. The usual domestic products are being replaced by electronic gadgets—games, computers, all kinds of machinery for home consumption—which has narrowed the market down to a specialized one and has done the very same thing with the demand for labor. The ordinary workingman, and working woman, is unable to compete in a highly technologized market. As a result, there is high unemployment because manufacturing is being done more effectively, and with far less cost, by machines instead of by people. It is the same problem that confronted the working people at the beginning of the Industrial Revolution. What is needed nowadays, in my opinion, is a cutting back of technology and a greater stress on production for domestic consumption.''

He surprised even himself, but it did seem a good theory. Wasn't it true that machines were replacing people? And it was also true that the emphasis on space technology, armaments material, electronics gadgets had undercut the validity of the man—and woman—in the street, who had no specialized knowledge but who encouraged the manufacture of the very products that were making humans obsolete by slavishly buying them.

The five women at the table had been whispering in low, excited voices among themselves. And Justin felt apprehensive. Damn it, he thought it was a pretty good answer to a very far-reaching question. Were they going to send him back to his cell to have his balls busted?

He was very relieved when the whispering stopped, and Madame Chairwoman gave him her very first genuine smile of the evening. "You have done very well, Dr. Weston. We will be quite finished with you once you have responded to Madame Secretary of the Treasury."

Well, he was glad to hear that. He looked at the very beautiful blonde who occupied the chair at the right-hand end of the table. He remembered the texture of her pussy, the way it grabbed his dick like strong hands, squeezing the sperm out as though she was milking him.

"What do you think about money, Dr. Weston?"

He decided to try humor. "I just wish I had more of it," he said, with a charming smile. How could he answer an asshole question like that?

The women were smiling too; they seemed to like what he'd said.

Especially Madame Secretary of the Treasury. "Wouldn't we all, Dr. Weston. But I am talking about the international monetary system. As you very well know, perhaps two-thirds of the world is wrestling with bankruptcy, however undeclared, while the other one-third is handing out credits, lending money, and reeling under a completely disordered financial system. Do you have any ideas about how we might restructure the international monetary system? Do you think, for example, that it is good business for the U.S. dollar to continue as the standard of exchange?"

He nodded thoughtfully. "I see where you're going," he said. "Well, even the United States is aware that an expensive dollar cuts into our own prosperity. It calls for high interest rates, which makes the borrowing of money expensive and also undercuts the competitiveness of American products on the world market. At the same time, the answer seems to lie in greater productivity and in greater buying. Which means that we are wrapped up in a vicious circle inside of which high unemployment, costly money, international tensions, and all the other problems that confront us, can ultimately only be resolved by international cooperation. We must get rid of these tensions before we can safely think about whether the dollar ought to be the standard of exchange, or gold, or the petrodollar, or what have you. So in the final analysis, it does narrow down to the fact that we must incontestably love one another. We must lay aside suspicions, and threats, and lies and intrigues. And truly try to cooperate with one another. If we don't do that, then we really are in danger of seeing the end of the world in our own lifetime."

And thank you, Mr. President, he thought sardonically. Although he felt pretty damned pleased with himself. He thought he had done a fairly good job on such short notice. If nothing more, the mad charade had forced him to organize his thoughts in a way that he had not done since college. The threat of having your balls jazzed by electric shocks is also an excellent incentive to pure thought, he considered. Maybe the same thing ought to be done to world leaders, he thought, smiling to himself.

There were more questions. About Reagan, Thatcher, Andropov—"Who the hell is Andropov?" he asked humorously. And there was general laughter; the Russian leader hadn't been seen in public for over a hundred days by then—the Western socialist nations, the U.S. intervention in Granada, sex before marriage, abortion, the Middle East situation. He answered them all well, to the very best of his ability. He felt the women warming up to him.

Until finally: "Thank you, Dr. Weston. You have been most helpful and most informative." It was the chairwoman. She seemed to be pleased, along with her colleagues. "Now you may go back to your cell. If all goes well, it is our opinion that you ought to be able to walk out of Riverview tomorrow, a free man. Thank you again, Dr. Weston."

He went back to his cell in a semidaze. He didn't know what all the questions were about. But . . . *a free man*? Did he dare trust the madwomen? He looked at Thelma, but she seemed to be somewhere far away inside of her own thoughts.

"Well, Dr. Carew," he growled, "how do you think I did?"

His voice seemed to bring her back to the antiseptic-smelling halls of Riverview Hospital. "Oh . . . I think you did splendidly,'' she said. But she was biting her lip, and that bothered him. He decided not to ask her about whether he could count on being free tomorrow. Although she seemed so distracted now—preoccupied? Frightened, perhaps?—that he wondered if she'd even heard the chairwoman's last comment.

It was only when he was dining in his cell—the most delicious meal he'd had there, it consisted of giant shrimp stuffed with crab meat, a baked potato with chives and sour cream, and a giant helping of fresh spinach, with sour apple pie for dessert, and strong, black coffee—that he realized that Madame Chairwoman had not asked him a single important question.

And then he fell into a drugged sleep. That it was drugged came to him from inside the sleep, like little elfin voices screeching, "You're drugged! You're drugged!" into his drowsy ears. Yet everything that followed seemed so real that he found himself again doubting his own reason. A tall, beautiful woman came into his cell and gathered him into her arms in an agonized rush. He was always ready for tall, beautiful women, but this one made him uneasy even as she excited him. The moon was bright and staring, like a silver mirror reflecting light. He saw her raven-black hair, dilated green eyes, the sexy pout of exquisitely red lips, and the sharp glint of small white teeth as she pulled a kind of transparent shift over her head and stood naked and inviting in the moonlight. There was a quick kind of animal energy about her as she moved across the cell to his bunk where he lay sprawled naked and crucified by the daggers of moonbeams. She fell to her knees at the foot of the bunk, reached and caught the muscular slabs of his hairy thighs, parted them as she lifted him slightly at the same time, yawned over him, and took him deeply down into her throat. His body prickled with the heat of passion. He caught her by the hair and pulled her down harder on him, shivering as she finally resisted and released him, her breath rushing out in a great exhalation as her teeth nibbled almost unbearably around the head of his dick. Then in one fluid motion, she slid down his body, straddled his hardness, and guided him into her right up to the hilt. He felt her flat belly expand under his hands as she slid up and down on his bulk. A low moaning bubbled from her throat as she rode him in a frenzy, rising and falling on him, using her doubled-back legs as a spring. Her fingernails raked down his chest, burning him, increasing his passion. Suddenly, he was ramming into her, his hard buttocks tightened and thrusting, her own butt squeezed into his two hands. And he lifted her and slammed her brutally down on his dick, feeling it churn up inside the slick hot tube of her until she collapsed forward in spasms on top of him and he felt his own milk shoot out as she clutched and released him with her pussy, clutched and released. His own hot breath was sliding through his distended nostrils as she eased forward, still holding him, and he lifted slightly and met the slick hotness of her tongue, sucking it. Then, somehow, he was out of her cunt and in her mouth again. Her own belly was over his face now, the milk-white ass almost glittering from the moonlight as she squirmed down on top of him and his lips met the rubbery salty-sweet lips of her pussy and he sucked his own milk out of her while she sucked his milk out of him.

It seemed real and unreal at the same time. The guard at the cell gate was jacking off, face twisted and ugly with the voyeur's passion. There seemed to be other faces there, too—the women's committee that had questioned him in the therapy room. Dr. Porter. And Thelma's white face, wearing an expression he couldn't understand. . . .

It must have been later when he asked the woman,

"Who are you?" And she said, "You know me. You have always known me. I am Betty." And he said "Oh," feeling satisfied. Of course he knew Betty. He'd taken her virginity on the front end of the Model-T Ford back in Orlando that summer when he was fifteen.

So that's why Thelma was here. Thelma had planned it all. He remembered that Betty had eaten worms, and told her so. "I didn't eat worms," she said, smiling. "I said that to keep those horny southern boys away. But I liked you the minute I saw you—I loved you. So I got Thelma to set the whole thing up. It was wonderful. I'll never, never forget you. . . ."

Her arms held him like warm snakes, slithering around him. He remembered that long-ago night, the moon like this one; the two boys, the black and the white, how they'd jacked off each other's bony dicks. And how he'd withdrawn from Betty for the only time in his life, the sperm shooting out of him in a thin happy stream.

"I am Betty," she said, with a cryptic smile. "Andrea McKay for President!" And went away, a white wraith in the white moonlight.

And then he was partly awake, lying there in a pleasant daze, feeling hot water and gentle warm hands bathing him. The deep scratches on his chest burned as the hot, soapy water washed him there. And his dick, still partly erect, felt used, bitten, bruised. He had not dreamed at all.

FOUR

Dream or not, the sensation continued, a kind of disembodiment, as though he was living underwater. He was aware of being washed, dried, lifted, and dressed, like an oversized baby or a piece of fabric being handled in a dry cleaner's. Unmistakably, Bob Dante was there. And Thelma. Another unidentified person.

"God, he looks like hell. What do you suppose they gave him?"

"A hyponitrous acid compound." Thelma's cool, efficient voice. "The effect should wear off in a few hours."

"We don't have that much time, Dr. Carew."

"It would be best for the drug to wear off naturally, Mr. Dante. To give him an antidote now would just prolong the agony, so to speak."

Light and sound came at him in blurs and flashes. He felt Bob Dante's arms around his waist, his shoulder, carrying him along as though he were a casualty—Bob Dante's distinctive smell of pine needles and bay rum, always on the hunt for women.

And then, that other man's voice. "God, I feel so

responsible for this! If I had only known that it was top-level government business. . . ."

"I thought we agreed, Peters, that you'd keep your mouth shut." Dante's voice was hard, dangerous. "You haven't seen anything, you don't know anything."

"Ah . . . yes . . . of course."

Bob Dante had come into the picture. And Peters. Yes, Joel Peters. The newspaperman from Carlton, Illinois. Andrea McKay's hometown, Peters had said. And now, thoroughly intimidated by Bob Dante.

"We'd better take some blankets along," Thelma said. "He seems to be shivering. That is one of the side effects of the drug."

He felt blankets draped around his shoulders, as though he were an old horse.

"Let's go." Dante again.

He felt himself moving, although he was unaware of his legs functioning. Like being drawn along on some kind of platform. A float. A float in a Thanksgiving Day parade.

He saw two faces that he recognized. The guards who'd menaced him with their peters. Moving in that same slow-motion way, he turned and cold-cocked one before anyone knew what was happening. As the other one moved forward, clawing for his gun, Justin gave him a beautiful kick in the nuts.

"He'll be all right. Those guards must have given him a hard time." Dante's voice held a grin in it.

"Let's get out of here!" Thelma's voice was sharp for the first time. A woman under pressure; Justin wondered how long it would take for her to break. "They responded very well to the legal papers to get him out of here. But who knows how long they'll stand for this? We've got to move him, and *quickly*!"

Now he was moving quickly, the parade float being speeded up. His legs were moving; he went down corridors, down stairs, out into pale sunlight that smacked him in the face like a soft yellow fist. Spring slid into his nostrils like a magic aroma.

Then he was stuffed into a car, where he suddenly felt exhausted. He fell asleep on someone's shoulder—Dante's—with someone's arm's holding him erect—Thelma's—her breast hard and urgent against his arm.

When he woke up, he felt better, almost normal. The sensation of swimming had decreased and his head felt clearer, but larger and aching, as though he'd been hit by a steel beam. Wide-awake, but lying perfectly still, he inspected his surroundings through slitted eyes.

Lying full length on a comfortable bed, he was in the passenger section of a small private jet in flight. Across from him, slouched in an upholstered leather chair, Bob Dante dozed with both hands trapped protectively in his crotch. Five or six feet away from Dante, Thelma Carew and Joel Peters drank coffee, in the middle of urgent conversation. The jet sliced quietly, cleanly through the air, the whine of its engine blotted out by soundproofed paneling.

"I'm afraid I don't know any more about this than you do," Thelma was saying to Joel Peters. "Dr. Porter called me to his office first thing this morning and told me I was to cooperate with Mr. Dante there in every way I could."

"He's from the CIA," Joel Peters said, looking around cautiously. "I suspect that the other one is too. The one they call Dr. Weston. If he's a doctor, then I'm a pelican. They both look like killers to me," he added confidentially.

Thelma laughed, but it came out somewhat shakily. "Well, I *am* a doctor, Mr. Peters. And a psychiatrist as well. If there's one thing you learn in medical school, it's not to judge a book by its cover. Or people by their appearances. Furthermore, how do you know that Mr. Dante's from the CIA?"

"He showed me his credentials," Joel Peters said. He

sounded miffed under his mild rebuke. "I called Washington to verify them. He had an order from a federal judge in Chicago, a writ of habeus corpus for one Michel Dupré and a bunch of other aliases that the other one might be traveling under. The only name I recognized was Dr. George Weston. Then that Dante one showed me the photograph of Weston, and I carred him out to Riverview. They got my name from the report of the accident, that explosion at the tollbooth that I turned in to the state police."

He sipped from his coffee and nodded toward Justin and Dante. "I'll bet they're both from the CIA," he said spitefully, as though he had caught a trusted friend crapping on a prized rug. "This is a government jet, isn't it? And those are government pilots—no need to look surprised. I asked. After all, I am a journalist, you know. I pledged my cooperation only if they let me tag along. But what are you doing here, doctor? Are you also with the CIA?"

Thelma smiled pleasantly. "Heaven forbid! I'm only along as a medical escort, in case of emergencies." Then she leaned toward Joel Peters, and her voice was low and confidential when she spoke. "Dr. Weston, or whatever his name is, has been temporarily released for humanitarian reasons. He had an aunt in Orlando, Florida, who is on her deathbed. That's what the court order is all about, Mr. Peters. And I happen to know that the aunt is quite ill, and not expected to last the day. As for all the CIA nonsense, I suggest that you've been reading too many spy novels."

"Perhaps," Joel Peters said. He had been successfully sidetracked from the CIA by the information about the dying aunt. "I'm really sorry to hear that," he said. "You know, I live alone with my invalid mother. A neighbor's looking after her while I'm away. But Mother's going to have to go too, one of these days. And I dread it! I simply don't know what I'll do if Mother dies."

"Life has a way of going on," Thelma said. And she sipped her coffee while Joel Peters apparently wrestled with the torment of his own thoughts at the prospect of being left motherless.

As for Justin, the news about Aunt Eugenia had torn at his heart. So, she was dying. It saddened him, but it was not a surprise. She herself had prepared him for the eventuality of her death in various letters that she wrote him. "I'm just an old woman," she'd said. "Dying is not all that bad, I'm sure. So many others before me have gone through it that I do not think it is something we should be afraid of. It is the churches, the undertakers, and the cemetery owners who slyly keep us in terror of it so that they can be certain to make their profit. But I do sincerely believe that the condition called death is merely a continuation of the condition that we call life. When my time comes, dear, you must not grieve. You and your son must go forward, to your own individual or separate destinies. I would be very disappointed to think that you had done otherwise."

He stirred on the makeshift bed to let Thelma know that he was awake. She came over and checked him professionally—his tongue, throat, eyes, muscle reaction, heart, respiration, and blood pressure. "I'd say you're just fine," she said. She touched his hand and smiled. But his hard blue eyes stared coldly at her as he pulled his hand away. He still didn't know what her part was in all of this. Joel Peters smiled at them from his perch, then turned to look out the window.

Bob Dante was also awake. "God, you're all right, Justin? I'm glad, old buddy! I couldn't be happier!" Dante's enthusiasm was go genuine that Justin found himself relaxing as Dante went on. "They obviously put you through a wringer back there in Riverview. But you seem to have stood it pretty well." He slapped Justin fondly on the shoulder; then his handsome Italian face turned serious. "I guess you know about your aunt?"

"No. What has happened to her?"

"She's been poisoned, Justin. She's not expected to live. That's why we had to spring you from Riverview. The poison's all through her system. It was too late for an antidote when we found her. Even if there was one."

"Who did it?" Justin said coldly.

Dante shrugged, as though the answer ought to be apparent. "SADIF," he said.

The Old Man was waiting for them at the airport when the plane landed in a sudden heavy rainstorm. "Hello, Justin. Good to see you again." He took Justin off to one side, out of hearing of the others.

"How is Aunt Eugenia?" Justin asked. He wanted to knock the hell out of the Old Man, to ask him how it was possible for the CIA to fuck up so many times. First with him in the asylum, and now they had lost Aunt Eugenia to SADIF. But there'd be time to settle those accounts later. "How is my aunt?"

The Old Man looked grim. "Your mother is very grave," he said.

Justin looked at him in amazement. "My *mother*? You mean Aunt Eugenia, don't you?"

"She's really your mother, Justin. You'll have a chance to talk to her. She's very weak. But I wanted you to be prepared for the truth. SADIF, those son of bitches, poisoned her."

Walking out of the airport to the waiting limousine, Justin forbade himself from giving over to his thoughts as the party drove through the sweeping rainstorm to Aunt Eugenia's white clapboard house.

"Well, the time has finally come," she said in a weak voice, giving him a small smile after he'd bent to kiss her cheek. "I can't say that I am completely unhappy. Indeed, it gives me the opportunity to finally tell you the truth, and I welcome that. You see, dear, I am really your mother. Shall I tell you about it?"

He swallowed hard, quickly. "Please," he said. "I'd like to hear, if it wouldn't tire you too much."

Her color was all wrong, a kind of pasty gray. She kept trying to wet her lips with the tip of her tongue, until he held a glass of water from the bedside table for her to take a few sips through a straw. Soon, the Old Man had said, the poison would tighten its grip around her old heart like a steel fist. How had SADIF got to her? And why?

But for the moment, he wanted to hear her explain how it happened that she was his mother, masquerading as his aunt all these years. "You're sure you want to talk?" he asked.

"I am far too excited, too happy, *not* to talk," she said. "Besides, it's a story that I've wanted to tell for so many years that I know it by heart. Bring your chair closer. And listen. Perhaps you will understand why your father and I decided to deceive you, whom we loved more than anybody else in the whole world."

It was indeed an unpleasant story of deception and greed that she told. Engaged to marry wealthy Anna Mason, of the Rochester, New York, Masons, Major Adam Johnson, a career officer in the U.S. Air Force, had met Eugenia Martin on a romantic weekend and had fallen in love with her. Or thought that he had.

"I was never one who paid much attention to social or moral cliches," Eugenia Martin said. "Whether your father loved me or not was quite unimportant to me. I did not love him, but I wanted a child by him. 'No strings attached,' I told him. He seemed to me to be a fine physical and mental specimen, and I've never regretted the choice."

She coughed slightly and struggled to sit up. Justin arranged the pillows behind her and held the water for her again.

"I suppose I might have been the original liberated woman," she went on. "My family were sturdy Virginia farmers with hardly a penny to their name. But I wanted something more than the desperate poverty we grew up in. So I left the farm and went to college, and came out with a degree in business administration. At any rate, all of this is written down for you in a document with my lawyer. I only wanted to give you some of the background so you might understand why I wanted the benefit of having a child without all the other meaningless complications of married life.

"When your father found out that I was indeed pregnant, he began to act like any other man. He wanted to marry me, while he was already practically married to Anna Mason. He wanted to make me an 'honest' woman, whereas I did not feel that I had done anything especially dishonest. I was finally able to convince him that he ought to forget about me and the baby I was carrying. I'd managed to save some money of my own; I'd already prepared a story about my husband having been killed in the war—it was 1947, and there were many war widows to comfort one another. If nothing more, Adam's being married to Anna Mason and all her millions would further his career. He agreed to go through with the marriage only on the condition that we not lose contact, and that I accept help from him.

"Well, I agreed. And that turned out to be a bigger mistake than it seemed at the time. It was because of those payments that Anna found out about your birth and my relationship with your father. And she used it cleverly to her own advantage, as she used everything and everybody. She wanted a son—by the time she squeezed the truth out of your father, you were barely nine months old—but she didn't want to go through the trouble of having one of her own.

"It would ruin her figure, she said. And would probably be a big bore, so your father reported to me. But he was frantic for a child; they had even considered adopting one. Then Anna found out about your father's payments to me and got the rest of the truth out of him. He was always helpless in her hands, which is why she was able to drag him into this SADIF thing that finally brought about the destruction of them both.

"At any rate, she applied tremendous pressure. She threatened to make the whole thing public, which would have ruined your father's career. I finally agreed to give you up to them. But I demanded some conditions as well. That the money keep on coming was one of them. I wanted it for you, and it certainly didn't matter to Anna, since she had plenty of it. The other condition was that I would be your aunt Eugenia, and that you would come to visit me from time to time. Of course, I agreed never to breathe a word to you about who I really was. And that worked out fine.

"Anna had never met me, but your father convinced her that I was his sister. At least, she appeared to be convinced, or didn't care to think otherwise as long as she had you. We met on several occasions, and she cut me dead. My own feeling about her was that she was a very domineering and disturbed woman. She made your father's life a hell. I'm sure that you also suffered at her hands, my dear."

Her narrative was frequently interrupted by fits of coughing which wracked her thin body. Now, she reached out and grabbed Justin's hand; her eyes seemed lit by a terrible inner fire. "Can you ever forgive me, my dear? I wanted the best for you, and for myself as well. I am not going to lie and pretend that everything was done for your benefit. I also benefited. But I did sincerely believe that you'd be better off with Anna and your father than you would have been with me. I know my good parts, and I know my bad. I would have been a terrible mother. I think that I served you much better as an aunt."

Again she was interrupted by spasms of coughing, which brought a plump, freckle-faced nurse to attend her. "Would you mind stepping outside for a few minutes?" the nurse said, preparing a syringe. "I've got to give her a shot in the hip." Justin was glad for the diversion; it gave him time to go out with the others and to gulp down a drink.

"How is she?" the Old Man said; he seemed genuinely worried.

Justin hesitated, fighting his emotions. "She's dying," he finally said. "It might happen in the next few minutes." He felt tears burn his eyes and turned away to the fireplace, where small logs were burning cheerfully. Outside, the rain slashed against the house; he felt that there was a sense of dampness and desperation to everything.

Dante stood at the fireplace, an arm propped on the mantel. Thelma and Joel Peters sat together on an overstuffed sofa, looking rather like chastened schoolchildren. Justin stared into the fire, clenching and unclenching his jaw. "How long have you known about her?" he said. The question was clearly aimed at the Old Man, standing behind him.

"From the minute we took you on in the Agency," the Old Man said. "As you know, your father was involved with intelligence affairs on the National Security Council. When we ran a check on you, it meant that we had to go into his personal files and papers. They were open to us, after his unfortunate death. A letter was found there, addressed to me. General Johnson and I had known each other for many years. He entrusted the information to me, asking me to use it only when the necessity arose. That's why we got you out of Riverview. It seemed necessary."

The nurse came out. "You may go in now," she said. The look on her face told them that Aunt Eugenia's time was running out.

She talked with more difficulty now, her breathing irregular and labored. "Do you forgive me, son?"

It was more than he could bear. He sat on the bed and gathered her so frail body into his arms. "There is nothing to forgive," he said, rocking her tenderly. "I always wished you were my mother, whenever I came to visit you."

Her thin arms crept up his broad back. "What . . . what a very generous thing for you to say." Her cheek against his felt wet, like fine old lace. "Sometimes . . . sometimes, it was very difficult not to tell you the truth. . . ."

"I know," he said. "I know."

He felt her body stiffen in his arms. "But . . . but you must be careful . . . careful of the girl. . . . The one who poisoned me. . . ."

Now he held her away from him, inspecting the glazed blue eyes. For an instant's shock, he saw his face in her own. "What girl, Mother? Who are you talking about?"

Her hands signaled for him to lay her back on the pillows, and he did so. He knew that death was not very far away now.

"A girl . . . a very beautiful girl. . . . She . . . she bothered me so much . . . after the summer you spent here. . . . You were fifteen. . . . I used to smile . . . to smile whenever Thelma went up to your room. . . . Thelma has turned out very fine . . . hasn't she? I mean . . . a doctor and all. . . ."

"Yes, Mother. Now, tell me about the girl. Who was she? The one who poisoned . . . ?"

"The girl . . . a very beautiful girl. . . . She came here many times . . . wanting information about you. . . . She said she loved you. . . . She frightened me, so intense, so beautiful, so *strange*. . . . Of course, I told her nothing. . . .

Then she became vicious . . . violent. . . . I chased her away . . . I threatened to call the police. . . . That frightened her. . . . Then . . . two days ago . . . three days perhaps . . . I heated my milk . . . my milk I drink before I go to bed. . . . I left it to cool on the sideboard, as I usually do. . . . You know I like to drink it in bed . . . it helps me to sleep. . . .

"But . . . but it tasted funny that night . . . you know? . . . *strange* funny. . . . Then, the pain began . . . and she was standing over me . . . her face . . . her face full . . . full of *hate* . . . not beautiful anymore. . . . *I've poisoned you . . . you old witch.* . . . she said. *I'll find your nephew . . . if . . . if I have to look—*"

She gasped, sitting up straight, rigidly, clutching at his arms. Her eyes flared, then glazed over.

"Good-bye, my son . . . my . . . my very dearest son. . . ."

He leaned very close and said it into her ear: "Good-bye, Mother. I have always loved you. Always."

Her lips twisted in a brave smile. "I . . . love . . . you. . . ."

He lay her gently back against the pillows. His mother was dead.

The next few days were full of confusion and pain for Justin Perry. Following Aunt Eugenia's expressed wishes in her will, her remains were cremated and the ashes scattered to the wind. A friend had been selected to read lines from Shelley's "Ode to the West Wind" in a simple, dignified ceremony: "O Wind, if Winter comes, can Spring be far behind?" The undying optimism of noble men, nobly expressed.

Aunt Eugenia's will had named Roger Johnson, also known as Justin Perry, as her sole heir. "The total value comes to just a bit under eight million dollars, after taxes and the rest,'' the lawyer told him. ''Your aunt was a very shrewd businesswoman. She really worked hard at making her investments pay off.''

She did it for me, Justin thought, sometimes bitterly. Money had formed a solid triangle of circumstances in his life. Aunt Eugenia's early lack of it, which had pushed her to make it. The excess of money in Anna Mason's life, which had made her a spoiled snob. And the lack of money in his father's life, which had sent him gravitating toward Anna Mason and her millions; she had bought Justin's father a military career, and he paid her back by becoming her chattel and finally, her executioner.

Anna Mason Johnson hadn't left Justin one red cent, which he had hardly regretted. Upon her death, her fortune had been reabsorbed by the Mason family. Now, Justin assigned most of the money left to him by his real mother to a trust fund for his own son. As for himself, he'd go right on living has before, he decided.

The Old Man, Bob Dante, Joel Peters, and Thelma Carew had taken up temporary residence in Aunt Eugenia's house, to be near Justin and to lend support in the cleaning up of affairs connected with his mother's death. Still, they respected his privacy and left him pretty much to himself as he took long, solitary walks through the rain-streaked woods and windy fields, where spring was stretching out through the land like the flexing of large green and earth-colored muscles. He was trying to sort out his reactions to the startling, new revelations in his own life before he went back into the apparent confusion of Riverview Hospital, Aunt Eugenia's mysterious poisoner, and all the rest.

Aunt Eugenia's—his mother's—revelations to him had not been as painful as they might have been, because of the honest and tactful way she'd handled them. No tears, no apologies, no accusations. That he had loved her as his aunt, in life, made it easier for him to continue to love her as his mother in death.

The biggest problem had to do with SADIF, how they had managed to annihilate almost all of his family, real or imagined, like some Furies gone mad and concentrating on Justin's eventual destruction and the disappearance of all related to him. First, there had been Bambi, his wife. Then, Anna Mason—he found it very easy not to think of her ever again as his mother. Then, his father. And now, Aunt Eugenia.

Who was the "girl" who had worried Aunt Eugenia so much for information about Justin and then poisoned her so cruelly? SADIF, the Old Man had said. Dante had said the same thing. But how did they know?

Aunt Eugenia's land extended far out into the woods to the edge of a bluff overlooking a lake. Justin stood at the edge of the cliff, looking down into a gorge cut out by nature millions of years ago. He looked out upon the greening fields below, the low-slung, humpbacked mountains, the path of a creek where it sliced its way through the low ground.

He would keep this place, he decided, because it had belonged to Aunt Eugenia and seemed imbued with the quietness, the dignity, and the gentleness of spirit he had known of her in life. Nearby, a fat-breasted robin tugged backwards on sturdy legs at a stubborn worm. The cat eats the rat, the robin eats the worm.

Struggle is eternal, Justin thought, and reconciled himself. Now he would go back to his own struggle with SADIF and Operation Orlando. As he turned and walked back toward the house, a flock of white gulls—probably blown in from the nearby lake, or perhaps even from the sea—winged their way overhead in triumphant formation. And Justin Perry found peace.

*   *   *

Anticipating Justin's return, the Old Man had sent Joel Peters into town on some harmless errands after deliberately fixing the phone so that Peters couldn't make his daily saccharine calls to his invalid mother back in Carlton, Illinois.

Peters went reluctantly, but self-importantly; he was being chauffeured in a government car. "But I want to be back in time for the televised press conference with Andrea McKay," he said. "She's from Carlton, you know. You might say we're friends. And I want to call Mother from town. I don't want her worrying about not hearing from me."

Thelma had prepared a tray of sandwiches and a large pot of coffee. The fireplace was going, since a chill had set in from sporadic rain and gusts of wind. Justin, Dante, and Thelma sat around the coffee table; the Old Man stood with his back to the fire.

Looking at the Old Man's drawn face, Justin was almost willing to forgive him for so many recent foul-ups. He still felt trampled after nearly five months of being locked up in Riverview. And the poisoning of Aunt Eugenia ate at his guts. But he was aware that the Old Man had gotten rid of Joel Peters, by whatever subterfuge, because something was going to be discussed that the Old Man didn't want Peters to hear.

As for Thelma, she represented an enigma to Justin that he hoped the Old Man would soon resolve. Was she with the enemy? She might well be; it was not unusual for the Old Man to employ dark and devious tactics in order to bring the enemy to bay. Or she could be working for both SADIF and the CIA, without either organization knowing that she was a double agent. Although that could hardly be the case now, Justin thought.

She was curled on the sofa like a lovely kitten, the fire on the hearth matching the rich, red-gold of her hair. She wore tan slacks and a fluffy brown woollen sweater with a white turtleneck underneath. Justin had been polite but distant in his treatment of her during the past few days. But he wanted to know where she stood, damn it! Whose side was she on? Whenever her eyes met his, they held for a moment before she looked away. She had indeed grown into a fine woman, as Aunt Eugenia had said.

Dante occupied the sofa with her in his characteristic relaxed slump. Tall, gangling, completely unscrupulous, with dark Italian good looks, Bob Dante gave the appearance of casual aristocracy and an almost boyish appeal. Women always made the mistake of wanting to mother Dante. Until they suddenly found themselves in bed with him, surprised that the deceptive exterior masked a consummate cocksman. But Dante could be serious, and deadly as well. It was Dante who had brought Justin into the CIA after the death of Anna Mason and Justin's father's suicide. The two men enjoyed a deep, comfortable friendship. Each had saved the other's life on more than one occasion.

Now, the Old Man cleared his throat and began to speak, carrying them into the maze of Operation Orlando and of how it had brought them to the present point.

"This has been perhaps our strangest case to date," he said, "because we have been working actively in a defensive position while SADIF has been the aggressor all the way. What we are faced with here is a clear case of repeated provocations on the part of SADIF, provocations aimed at ourselves. In other words, SADIF very desperately wants us to do something that we very desperately do not want to do."

"And that is?" Dante drawled.

"They want us to go public with their present operation," the Old Man said. "And that is something that we can ill afford to do. Because we very strongly suspect that to do so would make things turn out exactly the way that SADIF has them planned to turn out. All that has gone on to date—and especially all that has involved you, Justin—has been a part of SADIF's plans to get Andrea McKay legitimately elected as the first woman president of the United States."

Justin eased himself around in his chair. "A woman president might not be such a bad idea," he said. "Unless something has happened in the early stages of the campaigning that I don't know about. Remember, I have been somewhat out of things since last November," he went on dryly. "The first and the last I heard about Andrea McKay, she had announced her intention to run for president. Has she gained any ground?"

It was Thelma Carew who answered him. "All polls indicate that if national elections were held now, in March, Andrea McKay would win the presidency, hands down." Thelma withdrew deeper into her sweater, as though suddenly chilled. "She has not made one single political speech; she has done no campaigning for her Federalist-Liberal party, in the usual sense. Yet she has an enormous following all over the country and is drawing strength away from the Democratic and Republican parties by poking fun at them. She eats baked rat, drinks California champagne, and is more popular than the Pope. Thanks to television and the press, Andrea McKay could very easily be elected president next November on a write-in ticket without even trying."

Justin stared at her in open disbelief. It was the Old Man who verified Thelma's statement as Bob Dante nodded agreement through slitted eyes.

"Thelma Carew is an old acquaintance of yours, Justin. But I'm afraid that you have not been made formally aware of her very important and loyal involvement with the CIA. We planted her in the Riverview Sanatarium last August, three months before we sent you there to find out what was going on. Using her position at Riverview as a cover, she has done some very valuable research on Andrea McKay, and her assessment of McKay's chances for stealing the presidency are, unfortunately, altogether true.''

''What the hell is going on?'' Justin growled. His face had turned mean. ''I feel as though I'm back in that goddamned asylum again. Has everybody gone mad?''

Now it was Dante who spoke, a soothing edge to his voice. ''It would seem that way, Justin, that everybody has gone mad. But what we are talking about is the manipulated madness of a very large and important part of the American voting public. Andrea McKay is a fabrication of the American news media. She is beautiful; she is brilliant; and she has successfully kept voters away from the primary elections by telling them not to go. 'Stay at home,' she croons, 'and vote for me in November.' If the present trend of absenteeism keeps up, and if the primary elections' stay-at-home voters do go out in November and cast their ballots for Andrea, then she will be elected president.''

Justin felt incredibly tense, and there was tension in the air as well. All eyes were on him as he wrestled with the implications of what the three of them had said.

So, Andrea McKay was a fabrication of the press—if anything could be said to be a fabrication of the press; the important thing to find out was where she'd come from before the press got its hands on her—a beautiful, charismatic woman who poked fun at both political parties and induced voters to stay away from the polls. Apparently, enough voters *were* staying away from the primaries so that everybody was getting scared that, come November, they would swarm from their homes and vote in Andrea McKay as president in a write-in vote.

That was possible, and Justin could understand it. An overwhelming popular vote for a third-party candidate could throw the political process into confusion, but not into chaos. Andrea could simply declare herself either a Democrat or Republican, then fuse her FLP followers with the party of her choice, go into the White House, and still function as an independent on most issues that were not in excessive conflict with the congressional majority. Party differences were not that profound in American politics, once you got away from the slogans and the mud-slinging used to attract the voters' attention.

Not a usual situation to contemplate, but certainly not an exceptionally dangerous one. So there must be something else at work that neither Dante, nor the Old Man, nor Thelma—he was glad to find out that she was on their side—was telling him.

"So, what is it?" he said. "You're not all doing flipflops just because some instant celebrity has found a way to manipulate the American public and to get herself elected president. And so what if she eats rats, or is a member of SADIF? We simply tell the American people, set the law on her ass, and that'll be the end of that. So what's the big deal? What is it that you're all holding back? And what is it that SADIF wants us to go public with, as you said at the beginning?"

He aimed his question at the Old Man, who lit a cigarette and drew deeply on it before answering. "Justin, let me digress for a few minutes before I answer your question. I want to know if you remember the comments I made about the press three years ago, before we changed our operational methods."

Justin nodded. "I remember very well. You came down hard on the press—maybe too hard, I thought then—although I'm sure the comments were justified. You were concerned about the danger of an irresponsible press shaping public opinion which would logically become irresponsible of itself. Or, at least, inimical and even hostile to the aims of government and its legitimate operations."

The Old Man smiled thinly. "I see that you do remember. Then you also recall that I talked about a hostile public that would become arbitrary to the point of saying that something was white only because the press said it was black. And vice versa."

"I remember that," Justin said. "You used the example of a bad politician being elected as a kind of rebellion by the voters because the press said he was good. And of a 'good' politician being elected because the press reports say he is 'bad.' You were talking about people responding in a completely contrary way because they no longer believe the truth of press reports and automatically go the opposite way."

"Exactly!" The Old Man slammed a fist into the palm of his other hand. "And that is why we cannot say that Andrea McKay is a SADIF agent trying to worm herself into the White House. Because the dumb fucking public wouldn't believe a word of it and would vote her in! Hell, they're ready to vote her in just because she's so damned beautiful and appears on TV talk shows. And they sit on their asses at home because she tells them to. Imagine what would happen if we came out and said that she's the enemy, that they ought not to vote for her, that she ought not to be president?"

Justin felt stunned. "They'd vote for her," he said. "The assholes would really vote for her."

Now he saw how devastating the Old Man's theories could be in actual practice. And for the CIA to expose Andrea McKay as a SADIF agent would only make her more attractive to a silly, ignorant, hostile, and arbitrary public. Especially if it was said that she was being smeared by the CIA.

The three of them were watching him intently. "I get your point," he said quietly. "So what can we do about Andrea McKay?"

The Old Man smiled, looked at his watch, and flipped his cigarette into the fireplace. "Well, for the time being, we can eat sandwiches, drink coffee, and listen to her on television." He switched on the set. "She's having her first press conference ever. Up to now, she's only been on TV talk shows, things like that. But they've done a hell of a job on her in newspapers and magazines. Now they're going to let her do her stuff on national television."

"Joel Peters will miss the show," Thelma said mischievously. She was serving coffee.

"Yeah." Dante grinned, then bit into a thick ham sandwich. "He's probably still talking to Mama."

Moved by pure impulse, Justin went over to Thelma, took the coffee things away from her, and tugged her lightly to her feet. "I'm so damned glad you're on our side," he said, wrapping his long arms around her. "I couldn't really be sure, back there in Riverview."

She wrapped her arms around him. She smelled fresh and fragrant, as though she had bathed in crushed violets. "You weren't supposed to be sure," she said. "You might have given something away. They were using the very best drugs to get you to talk."

"And I didn't."

"You didn't," she said, then laughed. "Not about anything important. Not about anything they understood."

"And you did?"

She laughed even harder, pulling away from him. "I did. You talked about sacrificing girls, and about virgins who eat worms."

Her eyes were rich with amusement, and he forced himself to smile. Although he felt a strange crawling along his spine. He was not sure that Thelma ought to be amused, although he could not say why, or why he felt a great sense of dread and unease invade his body.

But then it was time to listen to Andrea McKay. They

103

sat down to watch, munching sandwiches and drinking steaming hot coffee.

A good-looking announcer with the mandatory over-scrubbed look, Establishment haircut, and large white teeth came on the small screen. "Good afternoon, television viewers. The combined television networks are privileged to bring you today a special-events program in the public interest. Today Andrea McKay meets the press. There is certainly no need for me to tell you who Andrea McKay is. A recent *New York Times* poll has listed her as the most popular woman in America.

"In short, ladies and gentlemen, Andrea McKay is a modern-day phenomenon. A newcomer to the political scene, she has amassed a tremendous public following by a fresh, new, and highly provocative style that threatens to revolutionize American politics and to throw the nation's highest office into Andrea McKay's lap.

"Yet, by her own admission, Andrea McKay is not political. Since her entry into the presidential race barely five months ago, she has captured the public and disconcerted both major political parties by her unorthodox and freewheeling style. Public-opinion polls give Andrea McKay a commanding lead over both the Democratic and the incumbent Republican presidential candidates if elections were held today.

"Andrea McKay has come out of relative obscurity to turn the American political system upside down. Candidates for office are running scared, while Andrea McKay and her Federalist-Liberal party ridicule them, their fears, and the very system that she most likely will preside over as America's first female chief executive, and most probably the only third-party candidate ever to make it to the White House.

"But who is Andrea McKay? Where did she come from? And what are her ideas on the burning issues of the day? To find out the answers to these questions, the American League of Voters has arranged this encounter between Andrea McKay and five respected members of the press, in order to enlighten the American public as to what the phenomenal Andrea McKay is all about.''

"Sounds like a carnival," Thelma Carew said in a bored voice. She was sitting next to Justin on the sofa now, with Justin's arm comfortably around her shoulders. The panel of journalists was being introduced to the television audience. There were three men and two women to quiz Andrea McKay.

Bob Dante grunted. "I hope it's a fucking massacre," he said. "I hope they make her look like shit."

And the Old Man laughed bitterly. "Well, I certainly don't! Then we'll have *shit* for a president. Everybody will yell 'foul' if she comes off bad. Then they'll go out in hordes and vote for her in November, *especially* if she looks like shit."

But Justin still wasn't completely convinced. "You're really very serious about this, aren't you?" he asked the Old Man. There was still something unpleasant and undefined nagging at the back of his mind, but he couldn't quite put his finger on it.

"You're damned right I'm serious," the Old Man said, and he bit savagely into a sandwich.

Then they all fell silent as the camera zeroed in on Andrea McKay and the panel of journalists.

Justin felt himself tense. He broke out in a cold sweat. The woman on television was the same one who'd had sex with him in his cell at Riverview while he was drugged!

"My God!" he muttered. Thelma's arm seemed to tighten on his shoulders, and he forced himself to concentrate on the smiling woman's face in the television close-up.

She looked like a spectacular Dolly Parton with large breasts, black hair, and green eyes on the color set. Her

105

lips were red and provocative, her skin the color of ripe peaches. She gave the impression of being savant and slut simultaneously—the kind of woman who could be a buddy to a man or a woman, sleep with either one, tell dirty jokes with jolly good taste, get drunk without being obnoxious, slug it out with male or female, and yet maintain the healthy dimensions of her womanhood full and untarnished.

She seemed to be one of those rare women that other women seem to like, perhaps even to trust. She gave the impression of a shoulder to cry on, a secret to share, a tampon to be lent in the ladies' room. Her smile was broad, fun-filled—part sly, part ingenuous. From all appearances, Justin thought, she'd make one hell of a president. He could see why she had taken the American public by storm.

But what had she been doing fucking around with him at Riverview the other night? He couldn't be mistaken—the lump in his pants, throbbing at the memory, told him he wasn't mistaken. "I am Betty," she had said. "Andrea McKay for president!" Well, the Betty he'd fucked here in Orlando nearly twenty years ago certainly hadn't looked like that—although time could do things to a woman's face and figure. He remembered that Betty of the sacrifice had had stringy brown hair, but dye could have been used to change that.

She was dressed in a black-and-white polka-dot dress with a large black bow at the neck. With her healthy cheeks and high complexion, she might have been a beautiful wife sitting down for a brief discussion of world affairs, between vacuuming the house and preparing dinner for six. The camera stayed right on her, and she looked out at the audience through it with those wide green eyes filled with a kind of infectious amusement. She was, in short, a complete knockout. And then Justin concentrated fully as the press conference with Andrea got under way.

MODERATOR (smiling): Good afternoon, Ms. McKay.

ANDREA MCKAY (smiling): Good afternoon, Marvin. And good afternoon to the rest of you on the panel, as well as to the television viewing audience. (Loud applause from live studio audience.)

MODERATOR: Well, it certainly is nice to have you here with us, Ms. McKay. Although perhaps we ought to be a little afraid of you. . . .

ANDREA MCKAY (smiling): There's no need to be afraid of *me*, Roger. I might spark a little, but I certainly don't bite. (Laughter and loud applause from studio audience.)

MODERATOR (obviously blushing): Well . . . ah . . . that's nice, Ms. McKay. But I meant to say that we all ought to have a certain awe for you . . . *of* you . . . a certain . . . well, maybe *fear* wouldn't be too strong a word. After all, you have changed the course of American politics. According to the experts, you might very well be our next president. (Loud studio applause.) And now, Ms. McKay, we would like to ask you some questions for the benefit of our television viewing audience.

ANDREA MCKAY (smiling): I'd be very happy to answer any questions from you and the panel, Roger. (Studio applause.)

MODERATOR: Thank you, Ms. McKay. Ms. Geraldine Fishbein, of the *Washington Post*, I think I saw your hand first.

MS. FISHBEIN: Yes, Roger, I think you did. Ms. McKay, first of all, I'd like to say most sincerely that I consider it a great honor for myself and all of our sex to be a part of this very important press conference. You have really made waves in American politics, Ms. McKay, and I for one am certainly proud of you. (Loud studio applause, whistles, and shouts.)

ANDREA MCKAY (smiling): Thank you, Geraldine. I certainly do feel proud to be here myself, knowing that I am a symbol to millions of American women like yourself, who know now that there is an opportunity for them in American politics. This is a proud day for womanhood everywhere, and I am proud to be a part of it. (Loud and extended studio applause, whistles, and shouts.)

MS. FISHBEIN: Well . . . to get on with the questions I want to ask, Ms. McKay. What do you think should be the American stance in regard to nuclear weapons?

ANDREA MCKAY (looking thoughtful): That is a difficult question, Ms. Fishbein. You see, what we are dealing with here is an established fact that increases itself the more we wander around trying to find answers to the problem. If I remember correctly, the existing nuclear arsenal has enough firepower to destroy the world a thousand times over. That is the irrefutable fact. Both Russia and the United States are in the wrong, I think, when they refuse to recognize this fact. Indeed, it ought to be the basis for every round of negotiations that takes place in the arms race. But as it is, both countries talk of greater and greater deterrents, more sophisticated armaments, and all that sort of nonsense, as though the fact has somehow become myth. Of course, unilateral disarmament on the part of the United States would be as unthinkable as the same thing on the part of the Russians. . . .

She went on like that from question to question. It did not take Justin long to realize *that the phenomenal Andrea McKay was giving the same answers to the same questions that he had been asked by the five women at Riverview Hospital*! The panel of journalists had apparently been given a list of prepared questions to ask Andrea McKay.

As she commented on important world issues—every single question was the same as had been put to Justin; every answer was his, recorded for Andrea McKay to memorize and to pass off to a breathless public as products of her own mental processes—she might have been a television model doing several commercials at the same time. She frowned with an aspirin-proof headache—"Take Dristan, and see!"—moving on to the relief of a popular laxative, then to an analgesic to take the bite out of postmenstrual pain. Every American who had ever seen a commercial could identify with her as she discussed the defense budget, the Palestinian question, the unemployment problem.

She even stole Justin's humor and his jokes: "What do you think about money, Ms. McKay?" She dimpled, and those splendid green eyes seemed to drip with amusement. "I just wish I had more of it," she said, with a charming smile. As for her formula for a rapprochement between the Russian and the American peoples, it had also come from Justin, but was carefully edited for television consumption: "I think it was General Pershing who said that when people of different nations meet, they usually fight, but they always make love. The idea is his, but I have borrowed it because I think that it is very accurate. We ought to love one another. That is a very fine Christian concept."

Except for an uneasy tingling along his spine, Justin watched the show in apparent calmness, but only with one part of his mind. The other part was putting together all the unsaid things about Operation Orlando and was coming up with astonishing conclusions.

Andrea McKay had to be Betty, the girl he'd deflowered on the hood of the Model-T Ford over twenty years ago. She was also unmistakably the woman who'd come to him in his cell at Riverview after the question-and-answer session in the asylum. That session had been recorded—he'd heard the click of the machine being turned on—for Andrea's benefit, to give the public the picture of an integrated female mind digesting the great male-oriented issues of the day.

Andrea McKay had obviously been the woman who'd

hounded Aunt Eugenia, looking for Justin, and then had poisoned the old woman in a fit of anger and pure spite. Thelma Carew had been assigned to Riverview Sanatarium three months before Justin had been sent there . . . to find out what? *Thelma has done some very valuable research on Andrea McKay, using her position at Riverview as a cover,* the Old Man had said. *Her assessment of McKay's chances for stealing the presidency are, unfortunately, altogether true.*

Had Thelma done the evaluations on Andrea McKay in Riverview Sanatarium? Had Andrea been an inmate there? She was obviously a part of SADIF, according to the Old Man; did the SADIF raids on madhouses in Canada, the United States, and Mexico five months ago, where hundreds of maniacs were freed, have anything to do with Andrea McKay?

He was sweating now; his arm around Thelma's shoulders felt damp. He pulled it away, caught her face gently in his big hand, and forced her to look at him. "What is Andrea McKay's full name?" he asked.

The question, or perhaps the sound of his voice, seemed to startle her. "Her name is Andrea Elizabeth McKay," she said. "We called her Betty when you knew her."

He was aware that the Old Man and Dante were also looking at him. They seemed to know that he was working his way up a torturous trail of logic that had to end with one simple and devastating conclusion.

He could hear her voice droning on as she responded to more and more questions that were at least familiar to Justin. The answers were even more familiar. Andrea McKay was still following his script. He listened to her reel off his responses with a sense of growing horror.

Suddenly he got up and turned off the television set. A silence descended on the room, almost deafening for a while, until the vacuum was taken up by the whooshing of wind and rain outside, the crackling of the logs on the fire, as though the flames were smacking their lips around the wood with utter satisfaction.

"She's mad, isn't she? I mean, *she's absolutely fucking mad!*" he said, his whole body tense.

Not one of them said a word; and that was answer enough. He felt a fierce trembling in the area of his groin. His nerve ends seemed to scream. Taking a quick step, he lashed out with a closed fist and smashed the Old Man on the very point of his chin.

He felt Dante grab him from behind, started to knock hell out of him too, and then felt the violence subside as quickly as it had surged. Shaking his head in total disbelief, trying not to think of the five horrible months he'd spent in Riverview Sanatarium or of gentle Aunt Eugenia fed poison by a madwoman, he knelt gently and brought the Old Man to his feet.

"I'm sorry," Justin said.

"It's all right," the Old Man said. "If anybody ever deserved a walloping for what I've done to you, I do. But it couldn't be helped, Justin. We had to find out."

"I know," Justin said. He saw Dante eyeing him intently, apparently for another eruption of violence. Thelma had jumped to her feet when Justin hit the Old Man. She was also watching him speculatively.

"Well," the Old Man said, rubbing his jaw, "I guess that Dante and I can take off now. We'll leave you in the competent hands of Thelma. She knows all the details; she can explain them to you just as well as either Dante or I could."

Dante was still tense, uncertain. Justin reached out and pulled his friend to him. "I'm all right," he said. His body was trembling with anger and shock, but he was all right.

The Old Man had shrugged into his raincoat. "You're

suspended for three months, after this whole thing is over,'' he said, grinning. ''You can't go around walloping the boss without some kind of action being taken.''

That eased the tension. ''After this thing is over, I'll need three months' suspension,'' Justin said. He walked with Dante and the Old Man to the door. The rain was slashing down harder now; the three guards outside looked like drowned ducks.

''Let's go, boys,'' the Old Man said. And he dashed down the stairs to the waiting limousine.

Dante waited in the door with Justin for a few minutes. They lit cigarettes, standing shoulder to shoulder, as though the world outside offered a challenge that they had to meet together.

''Don't blame the Old Man too much,'' Dante finally said. ''It really was the only way, old buddy.''

Justin grinned. Now that he knew what they were up against—at least a part of it—he felt really fine. ''I know, Dante. Don't worry about me. Where are you and the Old Man on your way to?''

Now Dante grinned. ''We're supposed to be spies, remember? If I told you everything, then there wouldn't be any secrets.'' He punched Justin fondly on the shoulder and rushed down to the limousine. Justin waited until the two cars had pulled off; then he went back inside to Thelma.

It was an elaborate scheme, all quite unreal and very carefully planned, Thelma said. The first news about the plot had surfaced in Russia five years ago.

''I am married to a Russian, Justin, and have lived in Moscow ever since I graduated from medical school here in Florida. My husband's name is Sergei. He was also here studying medicine. He taught me Russian, I helped him with his English, and we fell in love. Sergei's father is an important member of the Politburo, which arranged for me to study in Moscow on a fellowship. I took advantage of it, and married Sergei. There was no family here to speak of—my father ran off from Orlando with another woman when I was twelve; my mother slaved to put me through medical school, and then dropped dead two days after my graduation. Sergei and I have two lovely children, one twelve, the other nine. I suppose that I'm as happy in Russia as I would be if I still lived in the States. I guess marriage is what you make of it, whether it's in Moscow or Florida.''

Her lovely eyes clouded over, and she turned slightly away. ''Although there are some things I do miss about not being in the States. I hate having to stand in line for everything. And the summers are all so short there; winter is sometimes beautiful, but mostly a nightmare for me. At any rate, I work in the state hospital, and also have my private practice. The system's all right for the Russians, I suppose, but I think the average American—and I've held on to my U.S. citizenship—would find it too closed, too regimented, and terribly suspicious. Sergei, my husband, is one of the real suspicious ones. He's a medical doctor, but he has many friends in the KGB. And that's how he heard about the SADIF plot to make a madwoman the American president.''

She smiled, remembering. She was naked, as was Justin; she stroked his thick black hair where his head lay comfortably at the juncture of her milk-white thighs. ''Everybody in the Kremlin absolutely flipped,'' she said. ''They had horrifying visions of America's nuclear-attack power and its foreign policy all being in the hands of a certifiable maniac. And a woman at that. Despite all their parading about and their huffing and puffing about sexual equality, Russian men are the world's most accomplished chauvinist pigs. I think that the fact of a woman being president frightened them more than her madness.

"The KGB, which is probably the world's most extensive and competent spy system, had picked up a lot of interesting information about Andrea McKay and SADIF's grooming of her to screw up the American political system. The Russians weren't too worried about any changes in our system, but they wanted it to be a change to communism. When they approached SADIF with the idea, they were soundly rejected. In retaliation, the KGB exposed to the CIA what they knew of the plot.

"The Orlando connection between Andrea and myself very quickly came out of the computers, and I was made a member of the KGB and was sent to the States on a lend-lease basis. The CIA put me to work right away, in your division with the Old Man as chief. Although I think that the KGB's idea was to have me as a kind of goodwill ambassador, to convince the American government that the mad plot was strictly SADIF's."

She smiled, and squirmed against Justin, reaching down to wrap her small hand around his hardness. "Also, Sergei wanted to get rid of me and pushed the whole exchange through, with the help of his miserable father. And I wanted to get back home for a while. I have no intention of abandoning my children. But the two governments have agreed that they can join me here, as long as I do what I'm told.

"Also, I was dying to see you, Justin. And when it finally happened, there was nothing to do but to keep up the act. I'd only been in the States three months, but it seemed like an eternity of waiting! And then you were there, and I wanted to tear my hair out, calling you Dr. Weston! But Riverview Sanatarium is bugged from top to bottom with listening devices. It is of course a SADIF cell; and with Andrea McKay there, the security is absolutely incredible. I was surprised that you got in so easily."

Now Justin smiled; her fingernails were softly clawing

his dick, which throbbed away from the sensation, then curved back again for more. "They intended for me to get in," he said. "Like the Old Man said, SADIF's role in this whole thing has been mainly provocative. They dangle bait under our noses and hope that we will bite. If Andrea is really elected president, it makes the whole American system look silly. And we look just as silly if it ever comes out that we've let a madwoman even campaign for the presidency, instead of being locked up like she ought to be. SADIF gets the best of the deal either way. As it is right now, we're fairly helpless. SADIF's like the school-yard bully, daring us to tell; and we dare not because it's such a colossal joke. It makes us look bad now, and we'd look even worse if their plans work out the way they want them to. The only thing we can do is to keep our guard up and to play it cool. We've got to keep on sparring and refuse to fall into SADIF's trap. The way things are now, the minute we expose Andrea, she'll become all the more attractive to the voters. I was sent to Riverview posing as Dr. Weston to try and get a line on Andrea. Nobody told me you'd be there—another one of the Old Man's cute tricks. But it seems that Andrea saw a hell of a lot more of me than I did of her."

Thelma nodded. "Yes, that is true. But they also needed you there—SADIF, I mean—to keep Andrea happy and cooperative. Her madness is a strange mixture of long periods of lucidity, interrupted by brief periods of total insanity, in which she is liable to do anything. The mad periods can last from five minutes to five hours, but rarely any longer."

"I feel sorry for her," Justin said bitterly. "Did SADIF fuck with her mind like that?"

He felt Thelma shake her head. "No. For a long time, I thought that the fault was really mine," she said. "Having sex with you that way really blew her mind, I thought.

Betty—or Andrea, I should say—came back to Orlando every summer after that year she met you. She came here looking for you. She even found out from the other girls where your aunt lived and came here to this very house, looking for you. I don't know what your aunt told her, but Andrea always came away very upset. It wasn't until I went on to the University of Florida to do postgraduate work that it occurred to me that Andrea was probably mad.

"As it turned out, I was right. The insanity is congenital and hereditary; both her parents died in madhouses. And you are Andrea's favorite fantasy. She remembers that you took her virginity, and she has spent the better part of twenty mad years trying to find you."

Suddenly he felt very weird. He remembered how she'd whispered, *I'll never forget you*, down in the cold water of the lake, the sharp edges of her chilled lips biting like small blades into his ear. It was frightening now to consider that she really meant it.

I'll never forget you. Andrea McKay for president, and Justin Perry as her stud.

The murky chiming of bells from a nearby church seemed to expand his dick in Thelma's hands, reaching right into his balls. His hardness gone wild, he flipped over, entered her in a long, gasping plunge. And found blessed peace.

I'll never forget you. If something wasn't done to blow Operation Orlando up in SADIF's smirking face, he thought, it would be a very long time before the American people forgot Andrea McKay.

FIVE

It was unusually chilly for the middle of March, and they drove with the car windows up, after flying from Chicago to Orlando. A Bach cantata was playing on the car radio, and Justin drove through the bleak Illinois countryside with a sense of relaxation that masked an inner tension trying to fight its way to the surface. Thelma sat beside him, apparently lost in her own thoughts.

Justin's own thoughts turned back to their last conversation about Andrea McKay. Thelma had really spooked him when she'd told him that he was Andrea's favorite fantasy. Since then, three days ago, Andrea McKay had haunted his dreams, and he thought unpleasantly about a female demon called succubus, out of mythology, said to have repeated sexual intercourse with men in their sleep.

"SADIF knew about your summers in Orlando. They even knew about that sacrifice nonsense with Andrea," Thelma had said. "This is a SADIF project that has been in the mill for a very long time."

Justin had nodded ruefully, remembering Anna Mason's leadership in SADIF. She had probably been a part of this project from the very beginning. The gutter tactics and sordid intrigue would have delighted her. And of course she would have known about Andrea McKay and Justin spending the summer in Orlando at the same time, even if only coincidentally.

"Go on," he said to Thelma.

"I feel terribly guilty about all of this," she said. "It's as though I played with fire that summer, and most of us wound up getting burned. Especially poor Aunt Eugenia, who had nothing to do with any of this at all. She was a very great woman, Justin. I never would have made it through school if she hadn't helped me. She bought me clothes, books, all the extra things a girl needs. My mother never could have done it alone."

Aunt Eugenia; his mother. He would keep it as a quiet, warm secret, even from Thelma. But it was a good secret, and made him feel whole again.

"Andrea poisoned Aunt Eugenia, didn't she?"

Thelma nodded. "But only because she was madly in love with you. She was trying to find you, and Aunt Eugenia frustrated that. As I said, I kept her away from your aunt while I was here during the summers. But after I went to Russia, apparently she really became a pest. I came to Orlando several weeks ago on Andrea's trail. She escaped again from the asylum and headed right for Orlando again, like a homing pigeon. She never forgot that first time with you."

He wished she'd stop saying that; it irritated him. He felt like a man with a corpse draped around his neck. "Did you see Andrea in Orlando then?" he asked.

"No, I didn't *see* her. But I knew she was there, from what Aunt Eugenia told me. We even thought about giving Andrea a phony address for you, but that would have only caused more trouble and confusion. Then, I went back to Riverview, and she showed up a few days later. A few days after that, she got out again. That's apparently when she poisoned your aunt.''

Justin grunted. "She seems to walk in and out of that place whenever she wants to. How do you explain that?''

"I can't." Justin shrugged. "Nobody can. Which I find very strange, since SADIF was preparing Andrea for her debut in politics there at Riverview, and she was watched like a hawk. Still, she escaped every so often and went to try and find you. As I've said, she appears quite normal for long periods of time. We are using a drug on her that keeps her pretty much under control, as long as it's administered regularly. But without the drug, she goes stark raving mad. After that, it's anybody's ballgame. She swings back and forth like a pendulum between madness and apparent sanity. She can be quite homicidal when she's in one of her moods. She was obviously like that the last time she saw Aunt Eugenia.''

They had made love again, had showered and dressed, and were sitting before the fireplace. The rain outside had lessened, but the wind was still howling around the house like noisy ghosts.

"Finally," Thelma went on, "you were sent to the asylum as bait to keep Andrea there, or to bring her back if she got away. We had a special viewing apparatus with which she could observe you in your cell without your being aware of it. And it kept her calm for a while. But her walking off whenever she wanted to was a very real problem at Riverview, before you got there.

"SADIF raided all of those madhouses last November to cover the fact that Andrea had escaped from Riverview. The Federalist-Liberal party, which is also SADIF, had just announced that it would participate in the presidential elections—nobody knew then their candidate was going to be Andrea—and then she just walked out of Riverview again.

"So SADIF decided to saturate all of North America with maniacs to increase Andrea's chances of not getting caught. As it happened, she wasn't. We still don't know how she did it, or where she goes after she gets out. She doesn't always go to Orlando, we know that for a fact. But it's all very mysterious. She stays as long as she wants, and then simply walks back in whenever she's ready to. I suggested that she be kept under restraint, but Dr. Porter vetoed that idea as though I'd prescribed poison. What surprises me is that nobody at Riverview really seemed very disturbed whenever Andrea disappeared, except for that first time, when they thought she'd get caught and blow the whole scheme. Personally, I'd like to know where it is that she goes."

Suddenly, unbelievably, Justin knew. "She goes to Carlton, Illinois," he said quietly.

At that moment, like an actor in the wings awaiting his cue, Joel Peters, the editor from Carlton, rang the doorbell. Justin went to let the round little man in. Peters was smiling, blinking behind his steamy glasses. "I got through to Mother fine," he said, folding his black umbrella and looking very pleased. "Mother wants me to come home. So I guess I'll be going back to Carlton."

"We're going too," Justin said quietly.

Joel Peters beamed like a happy hog, eyes masked behind the vapor on his glasses. "How very nice!" he cried. "Mother will be pleased to meet you both. And I'll make Chinese food." He wore a real shit-eating grin, like some smart-assed kid who's just been given a gold star in kindergarten.

He left for Carlton the next morning. It had stopped raining, the unseasonable cold had dissipated, and Orlando steamed under a sun as round and bright as a heated orange. Justin and Thelma wound up their business in

Orlando three days later and flew to Chicago, then rented a car for the last leg of the trip to Carlton, Illinois.

"Andrea McKay grew up here," Joel Peters said fondly, handing out gold-colored, reusable toothpicks to Justin, Thelma, and to the ill-tempered old woman in the wicker-backed wheelchair. "But Mother can tell you more about her than I. Mother was her teacher in high school."

They waited respectfully for Mrs. Peters to finish with her teeth. For a woman of apparent good breeding, she plied them with the diligence of a horse trader's wife. Whatever residue she found that threatened her old mouth with decay, she peered at it triumphantly on the end of the pick, then consigned it to a small paper coffin of Kleenex resting on her lap.

The four of them had dined on excellent Chinese food, a tasty mixture of almonds sautéed with thick chunks of chicken breast and an assortment of crisp vegetables snuggled up against the meat. They'd had fragrant lavender tea and were seated now in a small parlor in a kind of semicircle around Mrs. Peters and her toothpick. Justin and Thelma watched her uneasily, while Joel Peters worked at his own teeth like a monkey picking fleas, and with an energy similar to his mother's. Next door was the modest, one-story building where Joel Peters edited and published the weekly *Carlton Chronicle*.

The house where they sat in the parlor was also modest. On two stories, with enormous antennae sprouting from its shingled roof like the feelers of giant insects, the house was spare almost to the point of poverty. The old woman's bedroom, along with a kitchen, a bathroom, and the parlor, occupied the first floor. Upstairs were three bedrooms with another bath, Peters said. The furnishings they saw seemed to be from another age, in velvet, chenille, and massive old oak, as though two old ladies lived here, rather than one.

Justin and Thelma had sat in the parlor with Mrs. Peters while Joel had bustled about in the kitchen, wearing a frilly apron bright with designs. With his bulk, he looked like a small hippo about to toe-dance. As for Mrs. Peters, she was perhaps sixty-five, with sagging jowls, carefully wrought white hair, and sharp blue eyes that partly bulged. Her skin was the color of refined flour, with dabs of red rouge on her cheeks that gave her the appearance of an outraged circus doll. Her bright red lips were thin and pursed, obviously from years of disapproving, as though they wanted to disappear inside of her. "I always told Joel he ought to marry," she said, by way of conversation while they awaited the meal. "Then I would have a woman to wait on me. I am sometimes embarrassed when Joel does things for me."

She had talked very little before dinner and seemed to be nodding most of the time in her chair. Justin and Thelma sat in uncomfortable silence in the uncomfortable old chairs. Then Mrs. Peters's eyes would snap open and she'd drop a comment into the silence like a pebble flung into a well. "I had a stroke eight years ago," she said. "I taught history and civics at Carlton High School. One day, my whole left side went numb. I've been in this wheelchair ever since. I would prefer to be dead, but I'm too much of a coward to take my own life. And Joel is too full of mercy to take it for me."

"She was paralyzed for over two years," Joel Peters yelled cheerfully from the kitchen, "but we were able to nurse her back to health."

"Health?" The old woman harrumphed. She impressed Justin as being thoroughly disagreeable. In a similar situation, he would have gladly put her out of her misery. While she was covered from the waist down by a heavy woolen blanket, she had a thick neck and overly developed shoulders, as though she had spent time on crutches. "You call this health?'' she cried. Then, abruptly, she turned to Thelma. ''Are the two of you married?'' She used her voice like a rapier, and Thelma seemed to duck.

''No . . . no, we're not.''

''I don't mean to *him*.'' Her eyes raked Justin, then hopped away. ''*He's* not married to anybody. Are you?''

Joel had interrupted the inquisition by announcing dinner: ''Soup's on!'' They ate on an oilcloth-covered table in the small dining room, which smelled of dust and disuse. The food was surprisingly good. The old woman ate with great appetite, burping sometimes between bites. She had her own teeth still, and extremely strong jaws, the vegetables crunching in her mouth as though she cracked nuts. She seemed to chew each mouthful at least a hundred times, hunched pugnaciously over her plate as she apparently counted.

Joel Peters talked about Carlton during the dinner.' ''It's a very young town,'' he said. ''It was incorporated only in 1945, after the war. So many people had come here to work in the aircraft factory over the river in Springfield, that's how the town got started. The plant was finally phased out, but the people stayed on. We've grown quite a bit since then. The population now is a little over twelve thousand people. We've got a prosperous paper plant and an aspirin factory, which makes pills for all the American companies and stamps their individual names on them. We're not a poor town, but we're not overly prosperous either.'' He chuckled and wiped his tiny little mouth on a dingy white napkin. ''If you look on the map, you'll see we're smack in the middle of the Mississippi, with the river flowing around us. The north end of the island is below water level, so we've built a dike there to hold back the river. A bridge on either side of the island connects us to the mainland. So all in all, we're pretty happy here on our little island. . . . Will you have more, Dr. Carew?''

Thelma smiled. "Yes. Please. It's really very good."

"You sound surprised," Mrs. Peters snapped. Her jaws quivered like a pit bull's. "Joel is an extraordinary cook. Men are always the best cooks."

The old woman's every comment seemed an aggression. Thelma colored and ducked her head. She seemed strangely intimidated by the mother's presence.

"I've looked on the map," Justin said. "The island and the river flowing around it give the impression of a mud-colored snake having gorged itself on something very large."

Joel Peters laughed. "And Carlton is the morsel! Very good, Justin! Very good!" He seemed to be enjoying himself immensely.

But his mother cocked a blue eye. "There are no children," she said.

"Oh, Mother," Peters said cheerfully. "Are we going to go into that again?" He turned to Justin and Thelma, explaining. "Carlton has managed to achieve zero-level population since quite a few years back. No babies are being born. And if they are, the parents move out immediately for greener pastures. I'm afraid that Carlton isn't able to sustain the good family types we'd like to have."

"It's unnatural," Mrs. Peters grumbled. "There ought to be children around. *Small* children." The last seemed to be a definite dig at Joel.

Thelma ventured timidly. "It is odd," she said. "Children do make a world of difference."

"How do you know?" Mrs. Peters challenged bluntly. "Do you have any?"

"Two."

"Why aren't they with you?"

"They're with their father." For once, she stood up to the old beast.

"Ah!" Mrs. Peters sounded completely satisfied. "Divorced. I knew it. You have that discarded look about you." She went on chewing.

Mercifully, the dinner ended. They were now in the parlor. Mrs. Peters had routed out various pieces of the repast from her teeth and wiped them into the Kleenex coffin, as though she had found leeches. Justin was reminded of the pilot fish that keep the teeth of sharks clean.

"I was indeed Andrea's teacher," Mrs. Peters finally said after Joel had collected the toothpicks and his mother's paper coffin. "She was a very gifted student, quick and responsive. And a very pretty girl. I was not at all surprised when she announced for president. I would be extremely gratified if she wins."

"It seems that she might," Joel cut in excitedly. "All the polls say so. It seems that she has brought . . . *audacity* . . . to American politics," he ventured.

"I'd dare say she did." Mrs. Peters nodded thoughtfully. "She was audacious, I certainly remember that. When her mother died under mysterious circumstances, it was openly said that the father murdered her. Tom McKay, I remember him well. He'd been a student of mine thirty years before, when I was teaching on the primary level. A very likable man, but nothing remarkable. For years, he was foreman over at the aspirin factory, where they used to make airplanes. People said he killed the mother—her name was Mary. Mary McKay. As nice a person as you'd ever want to meet. Andrea stood up for her father against the accusations, but he never got over them, poor thing. He was found floating in the river up near the dike one morning. The coroner said accidental death by drowning. But it certainly looked like suicide. He'd arranged everything so carefully—insurance policies, bankbooks, a fresh will leaving a modest sum of money and a piece of property to Andrea. She was only around fifteen when it happened. She lived here with an aunt. Then I remember that she went off to Florida that summer for the first time. She had relatives there, and went each summer after that.''

Justin and Thelma looked at each other, then away; the summer Mrs. Peters was talking about was the one when Justin had taken Andrea's virginity.

''I did a story about the deaths,'' Joel said. ''About the mother, then about the father. Andrea seemed a girl haunted by tragedy. She went to Florida that first time and came back pregnant. It caused quite a few raised eyebrows in the town.''

Justin's face went white. ''Pregnant?'' It couldn't have been his doing; he had withdrawn from her, he remembered. The ejaculation had spurted onto the car. He noticed that Thelma kept her head slightly down, but seemed to be listening eagerly.

''There was a child,'' Peters said. ''But it died only a few hours after birth. A boy, I think it was. Wasn't it, Mother?''

Mrs. Peters nodded. ''It was a boy. A very handsome child. I went to see it shortly after it was born. Tom McKay did everything he could to protect Andrea from wagging tongues. But you know how those things are. And I think that her getting pregnant at that age did him more damage than anything else. He absolutely worshiped that girl. It wasn't too soon afterwards that he died. There was very good reason to believe he'd killed himself.''

Justin had a gut feeling that something was dreadfully wrong here, but he kept his voice calm as he commented. ''If any of this is found out by the press,'' he said, ''it might very well affect Andrea's chances for election.''

''Oh, I don't think so!'' Thelma said quickly. Somewhat too quickly, Justin thought. Why hadn't she told him about Andrea's being pregnant?

''The American public is a lot more educated, a lot more *forgiving*,'' Thelma went on, ''than it was twenty or thirty years ago. On the contrary, I think the true story about Andrea's life, and especially its tragedy, makes her much more human, much more acceptable to the voter. There is nothing we like so much as to be able to condemn, then to forgive. To do so makes us feel morally superior.''

Surprisingly, Mrs. Peters agreed energetically. "You're quite right, my dear. It would make her especially attractive to women. We know about suffering and deception. Don't you agree, Mr. Perry?" Her bulging eyes seemed wet with mockery. "You appear preoccupied all of a sudden. Joel, perhaps we could have our nightcap now. I fear that we've shaken up Mr. Perry's sensibilities.''

Why was the old bitch needling him? Justin wondered. *What did she know?* "I was only thinking," he said, "that perhaps you and Thelma are right, Mrs. Peters. My views are definitely chauvinistic. The voters do seem to like a bit of tarnish nowadays. What do you think, Joel?"

"I think they do. Scandal is the breath of successful politics nowadays.''

It struck Justin as odd that they were all in agreement—without knowing so, except for Thelma—with the Old Man's ideas along the same line. Still, he felt a nagging sense of unease, as though a sneak play had taken place right under his nose, without his even being aware of it.

Joel Peters had put on that ridiculous apron again—frilly around the edges, with carriages full of pumpkins and things in a repeated design. "Look at Teddy Kennedy, for example," Joel said. "The voters would have gladly elected him for president, not in spite of Chappaquiddick and Joan's divorcing him, but *because of it*. We're living in a very strange age. The new humanism, you might call it. Or the new hypocrisy. The sinner is far more acceptable than the saint and, rightly or wrongly, is perceived as being more honest and even worthier of trust than the one who has not publicly sinned.''

"Let him among you who has not sinned cast the first stone," Mrs. Peters said, in ominous tones. And then accepted her drink from Joel and swallowed the sweet, sticky anisette in one loud gulp. "I'm going to bed," she said abruptly. "It was so good of you to come, Mr. Perry, Dr. Carew. A very stimulating evening. Perhaps we shall have the pleasure again soon." Her eyes suddenly eclipsed, as though she had fallen into a stupor. "Joel."

"Yes, Mother." He hopped to, wheeled her around, and hustled her almost out of the room.

"Perhaps I can help." Thelma said.

Joel Peters turned and pierced Thelma with a look of complete reproach. "I am accustomed to handling Mother alone," he said stiffly. The starched apron around his waist stood at attention like an angry tutu. "Would you mind finding your own way out? I'm afraid this will take some time."

The pent-up tension of the evening exploded in Justin and Thelma simultaneously. They smiled agreeably, thanked Joel Peters for the evening, and gladly found their way out.

"What a horrible old woman!" Thelma cried, once they were breathing fresh air. The night was chilly, with a full moon sailing high in the dark blue sky like a golden galleon. As they walked past the offices of the *Carlton Chronicle* down Main Street, which sliced the island in half, they could see the tall masts of ships sliding past on the Mississippi. It was just ten o'clock, and the hour was struck somewhere near by stentorian bells, answered by the hollow horns of ships. There were only a few people out; "Carlton draws in its sidewalks after nine o'clock," Joel Peters had joked. The air was putrid with the smell of the river that washed around it on both sides, the serpent enveloping its prey.

"She is quite a monster," Justin agreed. "But the food

was good, and the talk was stimulating. At any rate, Joel seemed to enjoy himself."

Thelma linked her arm in his, the stride of her long legs matching his as they passed darkened shop windows on the way to the Carlton Hotel, where Justin had rented a room. Thelma was going back to her duties at Riverview, taking the rented car with her.

"I'd think they'd have little or no company," Thelma said, "not with that mother of his. He wags his tail around her like a little lap dog. She absolutely terrified me. *You have that discarded look about you,*" she said, imitating the old woman. "Can you imagine such rudeness?"

"I can, having heard it all night." Justin grinned. "And she terrified me too. That's why I kept my talk to a minimum. But it was interesting that the three of you agreed that Andrea's basic background will make her more acceptable to the voters."

"It will, Justin. And you know it. That's how things have become nowadays. Watergate marked the consecration of scoundrels. Do you see Richard Nixon in sackcloth and ashes anywhere, beating his breast and begging the public's forgiveness?"

"Maybe I'm old-fashioned," Justin said, "but I still believe in the ultimate good sense of the people, provided that they have all the facts. If I didn't believe that, I certainly couldn't be doing the kind of work I'm involved in."

She squeezed his arm and snuggled closer to him. "You're an idealist, and that's nice. But don't make the mistake of thinking there are many of you. In fact, I'd say that it's a dying minority."

He turned his head and kissed the tip of her nose; it was cold, like a healthy dog's is supposed to be. "And you're something of a cynic," he said amiably. "Look at the moon, the sky, the stars waiting just at the edge of the light. How can anybody be cynical about that?"

She laughed pleasantly. "Now you're being a romantic. My mother warned me about men who talk about the moon and stars."

They walked in quiet intimacy until they reached the dimly lit facade of the Carlton Hotel. It was an old, crumbling building that had obviously seen better days. A coat of paint would have done wonders for its peeling gray outside.

"Well, you've been escorted home," Thelma said. "Will I be seeing you soon?"

"I hope so." He wrapped his arms around her, pulling her to him. "Why didn't you tell me about Andrea's being pregnant?" he said.

He could feel the sudden violent trembling of her body through the thin coat she wore, as though a chill had passed through her. "I thought you knew." She pulled away from him and inspected his eyes. "You didn't know, did you? Oh, Justin! What a terrible way to find out. From that prattling old woman!"

Should he tell her that Andrea's baby couldn't have been his? And why was Thelma so convinced that it was? Had she kept an eye on Andrea every single minute of that summer in Orlando? Couldn't some other oversexed boy have gotten into Andrea's pants?

Thelma apparently mistook his silence as a signal for her to render more condolences. "I'm so sorry, Justin. I really thought you knew. Andrea thought so too."

That stunned him. "Andrea?" He clearly remembered her scared plea: *Please don't shoot in me . . . I'm afraid of getting pregnant.*

And he hadn't shot into her. Certainly . . . certainly Andrea remembered that. Or did she? Just how much fact could a madwoman remember when she was dominated by fantasy?

"It's all right, Thelma. Forget it. I was just surprised, that's all."

Thelma kissed his cheek, then his mouth. He responded automatically, almost coldly. "It's best that things turned out the way they did," she said, very professionally. She was talking about the child's death shortly after birth. "Insanity ran in Andrea's family, you know."

"I've been wondering about that," he said grimly. "You said back in Orlando that both of Andrea's parents died in madhouses. Yet, Mrs. Peters said they both died mysteriously here in Carlton. What's the gimmick?"

Thelma seemed very cool. "Have you forgotten Operation Orlando?" she said. "SADIF's side of it is the line that Mrs. Peters is following. But the truth is that Andrea's parents were both mad. They never set a foot here in Carlton. Andrea has never been here either, unless your theory about her coming here to hide out after she escapes from Riverview turns out to be true."

His lean stomach growled, as though more than the Chinese food was in open rebellion against his gut. "Go ahead," he said. "Tell me the rest of it." To encourage her, he leaned in against her and slipped his hand inside her coat. She wore a form-fitting woolen skirt; he reached down and rubbed the mound of her crotch. It was something he'd wanted to do all evening.

Giving a low moan of pleasure, she looked up and down the street, then leaned against him in the still night. Her hand slithered down and grabbed his dick, which swelled like a balloon at her touch.

"Carlton is a fake, a movie set," she said in a very rapid whisper. "Every single person here is a member of SADIF. It's a training ground for their new agents, a drawingboard for their new schemes. All that stuff that Joel Peters and his mother talked about is just plain nonsense, part of *their* script. Andrea McKay needs a hometown, a background laced with equal portions of scandal, tragedy, and respectability.'' She snaked her head backward, her eyes inspecting him with a trace of concern. ''You seem surprised, Justin. Don't tell me that you didn't know.''

He forced himself to be calm. Their hands worked at each other with increasing rapidity. Suddenly she shuddered, released him, then caught his hand as multiple spasms wracked her body. He had brought her to orgasm standing there in the street.

''Of course I knew about Carlton,'' he said. ''I just wanted to hear you say it. The whole place seems so peaceful, so goddamned middle-American normal.'' He wanted to get off himself, but it was apparent that she was all business again. ''Everything seems so perfect, I was about to believe the lie myself.''

''Well, don't,'' she said firmly. ''I know how hard it is to always be in the middle of mystery and intrigue. I've had my share of it in the Soviet Union, believe me. But sometimes it wears off on you; the hunter becomes the hunted, so to speak. The best example is the high rate of workers at insane asylums who become insane themselves.''

She dug in her handbag for the car keys, unlocked the door, and got in. ''When will I see you again?'' she said, pressing his hand to her cold cheek.

He felt like inviting her up to his room for a quick fuck but decided against it. He was fairly convinced that the Carlton Hotel would frown on that sort of thing. ''I'll call you,'' he said.

Except for the heat in his groin, he felt cold himself, mired down in new horror that threatened to overwhelm him. He bent into the car and kissed her. ''Drive carefully,'' he said.

''And you be careful,'' she said. She smiled and pulled off, waving back through the window before she took the turnoff for the highway out of Carlton and over the east bridge to Riverview Sanatarium, twenty-six miles away.

Then Justin walked slowly into the lobby of the hotel, his head full of disturbing thoughts. Chief among them was the fact that he was to be locked away for the next several months in a town of twelve thousand fanatical SADIF agents.

And it followed that if Joel Peters and his mother lived in Carlton, and were spouting the SADIF line, then they were SADIF agents as well. The massive antennae on their rooftop was the big giveaway. But why did the Peter need such urgent radio contact with SADIF headquarters in Munich, Germany? So urgent that they risked being found out by the powerful antennae roosting on their housetop like an upside-down grasshopper? They were playing with far more power than any ordinary ham radio operator ever needed.

"May I have my key, please?"

There was a stunning blonde behind the desk. He wondered what the hell somebody that looked like her was doing in Carlton, SADIF or not. Her hair was the fine color of cornsilk; she wore a tight-fitting pink dress that accentuated her fabulous complexion. She had very large breasts and a succulent-looking mouth. He was very aware that his goddamned dick was still hard. He was wearing a windbreaker and tan-colored trousers; had she seen it when he came into the lobby?

The amusement in her pale green eyes told him that she had seen. "Anything else I can do for you, Mr. Perry?" She handed him the key to his room, her soft hand brushing his with subtle invitation.

"Anything you want to do for me?" he said, flashing her with a lopsided grin.

She turned to check the big, ugly clock, giving him a profile view of her big breasts, her finely sculptured features.

SADIF sure did know how to pick them, he had to give them that.

"I get off at eleven o'clock," she said. "Perhaps you'd like me to bring you a nightcap, or something."

"I'd love for you to bring me a nightcap, or something," he said. He smiled and walked over to the stairs leading up to the third floor. He felt her eyes burning into his back.

It was twenty-five minutes to eleven as he stripped and went into the shower. And he thought about his last secret conversation with the Old Man as he soaped himself down and stood under the lukewarm water, letting it slam down over his head.

"On one very important level of this operation," the Old Man said, "Thelma Carew is the key to a lot that we don't know about. She checks out okay, but there're a few things about her that just don't wash. For one thing, she's just too goddamned good as a spy, considering that her primary training really is in psychiatry."

They talked in the limousine on their way to Aunt Eugenia's from the Orlando airport. The driver was a trusted, veteran CIA agent. "So how do we bring her out?" Justin asked. It pained him to think that Thelma belonged to the other side.

"I'm going to leave you in her hands," the Old Man said. "Just play along with her; give her a lot of dick, although I'm sure I don't have to tell you that. If she tells you about Carlton being a SADIF nest—and it damned well is—then she's definitely one of them. We haven't said a word to her, not to anybody, about that. So if she tells you, it comes from SADIF. And it means that she's definitely one of them, and they're dangling more carrots under our nose."

"Why?" He had a sense that the maze had taken more unexpected turns and seemed to be closing in on him, threatening to squeeze him into dreadful immobility.

"You ask *me* why?" the Old Man shrugged. "Who knows? Right now, you have as much information as I do about what's going on. But who really knows any goddamned thing in this whole mess? That's why I'm turning you over to Thelma Carew, hoping that you can make some kind of a meaningful dent in this mess. Thelma will fill you in on things that you already know. But put the screws on her, stick some dick into her. I've got an idea that she'll lead you back to Carlton. Remember, they've got their script all written too. As for your being in Carlton, I've got an idea they want you there as some kind of bait. And not necessarily for Andrea McKay. But if Thelma tells you that the whole fucking town is SADIF, then she's SADIF too."

Well, she'd told him. And now here he was in Carlton, standing under a hot shower with a big hard-on. And Thelma Carew was probably back at Riverview by now. It almost knocked hell out of him, like a deadly blow to the heart, when she told him about Carlton being a SADIF town.

Goddamn! He was almost on the verge of falling in love with her. Was there nothing real in this pasteboard world? And how long would he have to be here in Carlton, a nest of serpents in the midland of America?

The Old Man had some definite plans for Carlton, whether Andrea McKay won the election or not.

"It's got to be destroyed," he said. "And everybody in it."

They were out walking in the woods behind the house then, and Bob Dante had joined them under the cloud-swollen sky.

"We've got to hit them, and hit them hard," the Old Man went on. "They've got a whole city out there on that island, dedicated to terrorism and subversion. We've got to give them a warning so they'll never try that kind of damned-fool thing again."

"That's over twelve thousand people," Dante said quietly.

But it was Justin who answered him. "There are nearly four-and-a-half billion people in the world," he said, "and SADIF is trying to take over the world." But he was willing to wipe out Carlton for what Andrea McKay had done to Aunt Eugenia.

Now, standing under the shower, it was thinking about Thelma being with SADIF that really hurt him. More important, Thelma had to know now that he knew about her. Why had it been necessary for her to tell him about Carlton? Didn't she know that in doing so, she'd made herself a prime candidate for death? And why did SADIF want him stashed out here in Carlton?

Well, he'd find out soon enough, he thought. For now, he was thinking excitedly about the blonde from downstairs. He turned the water to hot, soaped and scrubbed himself, then turned it to invigorating cold.

His excitement died down, then rose again as he toweled himself dry. He brushed his teeth, then strolled from the bathroom drying his hair. And found the blonde already naked, lying on his bed.

"Hi," she said, smiling, twirling the passkey around her index finger. "I'm Fran Whittaker. Come on over here and let me take care of that great big thing."

He went over, and they took care of each other for most of the night. The sun was coming up when he finally fell off to sleep. And to restless dreams of a goat resembling him, staked in a jungle maze with his cock hanging out, bait for roaming beasts.

As spring turned to summer and then to early fall, Justin came to know the people of Carlton and even made friends there. He was a journalist gathering material on Andrea McKay, he said—indeed, he carried credentials from the *Washington Post*, and some of his pieces appeared there—

for a book on her if she became president, which seemed entirely possible.

People opened up to him completely. Everybody talked about the tragedy of her parents, their pride that a presidential candidate, and a woman at that, had come from Carlton, and were eager to forgive her the mistakes in her past life and the excesses in her present one.

Other writers and radio and television people came, but soon went, most of them complaining of a lack of hospitality, even an air of gruff menace in the twelve thousand inhabitants packed on the little island in the Mississippi. But they were outgoing and very friendly with Justin Perry.

He knew the sheriff, the judge, the town drunk, the town idiot, the town whore—she was not Fran Whittaker, the hotel desk clerk, but a stout, respectable-looking woman who was lead soprano in the Carlton Methodist Church choir—along with dozens of other locals who razzed him over beer in the Silver Dollar Bar and bragged about their experiences in whatever war.

Justin saw Thelma perhaps two or three times a month and managed to make love to her in the Carlton Hotel while successfully dodging further invitations from Joel Peters to sit down to dinner with his irascible old mother. On all of Thelma's visits, he asked her for information about what was going on at the sanatarium.

"Absolutely nothing," she would say, with a puzzled frown. "If I didn't know better, I'd think that the whole setup was legitimate. I'm absolutely practicing psychiatry! It's all very unsettling." Justin could have told her the same thing about Carlton; it too seemed completely on the level. And he was actually practicing journalism, which had been his major at Syracuse.

"What about Andrea McKay?" he asked her. "Has she been back to Riverview?"

Thelma shook her head. Her shining red hair seemed to

have gold flecks in it. "Not at all. And I find that really the most surprising part. But Dr. Porter and the rest of the staff act as though they've never heard of her. Even when she appears on television, they never make the obvious comments about her having been at Riverview."

Justin did not find that surprising at all. With the hospital being a SADIF enclave, they certainly wouldn't want it known that the highly celebrated Andrea McKay, SADIF's presidential candidate, had come from that particular madhouse. As for Thelma Carew, he made love to her with unfeigned passion, and she seemed to respond in kind. But he sometimes had the impression that they moved discreetly around each other, like two partners sparring until they would no longer be able to pretend. If she really was with SADIF—and the Old Man affirmed and reaffirmed that as a fact every time Justin called in to Langley, for reporting and briefing on a scrambled line—then he would certainly have to kill her someday. The CIA had long ago decided not to make prisoners of SADIF agents; there were just too many of them to house, and to feed at the public trough.

Summer warmed the town and seemed to give its small, winding streets a special magic. Ships going up and down the Mississippi tossed hoarse greetings at the town from friendly horns. The factories making aspirins and bond paper from pulp brought down to Carlton's docks by ships from Canada, sent out great streams of smoke that dissipated against the usually blue sky in smudges like charcoal strokes.

Justin walked the town, got to know its people, its sparse woods, the dike at the northern end of the island—Carltonians called it a levee, perhaps unconsciously making it smaller and less important than it was because of its ominous mission: to keep the island from going underwater—where lovers met in the cool summer evenings and roustabouts scooted noisily on motorcycles along the length of the imposing brick wall that held back the river on the other side.

As for Joel Peters, Justin spent a lot of time with him and even allowed a few of his minor observations to be published on the editorial page of the *Chronicle*. When it was absolutely impossible to avoid the occasion any longer, Justin ate with Peters and his mother and found the old woman to be surprisingly charming when the mood was upon her. Then Joel would put his mother to bed while Justin waited outside in the misting night; sometimes a fog rolled in from the river as Joel walked him down to the Carlton Hotel, past white clapboard houses and neat brick shops squeezed against each other like broad-faced children with lighted eyes, huddling in a brave stance against the humid darkness.

The two men had little in common—except perhaps that they were on opposing sides, and might wind up killing each other once this operation was over—and they talked of nothing things until Joel said good night at the hotel, Justin thanked him for the dinner, and each went back to his separate dreams.

Fran Whittaker was a frequent visitor in Justin's room. She was vivacious and all animal, almost shooting fire and smoke through her nostrils, like a beautiful dragon, clawing at his broad back and tight butt as he completely possessed her. "Honey, you are the greatest," she said, "the absolutely greatest."

She was tireless, simple, and completely uncomplicated, almost childlike in her gratitude that she had finally found a satisfying lover. She introduced Justin proudly to her younger brother, a handsome, browned, gangling, boyish-looking man of around thirty. His name was Randy, and he wore a pleasant grin whenever he saw Justin. He had an unruly shock of chestnut-brown hair and his sister's pale green eyes. Fran told Justin that she'd once had sex with Randy. "It was nothing serious," she said. "We were really just kids. It felt good, but I'm not particularly into incest."

The town's usual sleepiness was disturbed late in August when a team of scientists concerned about the environment showed up from the U.S. Ecological Services. They brought trucks and motorboats and collected soil and river samples from on and around the island. Justin became particularly friendly with the group's chief. Tall, lanky, deceptively muscular, he called himself Dr. Eric Lindstrom. He had sun-bleached blond hair and a matching full beard and thick mustache, which gave him the appearance of a rather young Santa Claus. Townspeople could see Justin and Dr. Lindstrom out fishing for cats on the bobbing river, or drinking beer and smoking cigarettes in lazy conversation down by the levee. Joel Peters did a write-up on the ecological team, which was checking for levels of contamination in the Mississippi River and its environs. A week before they packed up and left, in the middle of September, a cargo ship heading downriver suddenly veered from its course and ran aground just a few yards south of the western bridge. Divers from Chicago and dour-looking repair ships scuttled around the grounded vessel for a week before it was finally floated. Carltonians stood on shore and cheered as the cargo ship swung free and hooted its way downriver.

But the main mood of the island, during that summer and early fall, had to do with Andrea McKay's progress in the election campaign. She still maintained an astonishing lead in the polls as the FLP's write-in candidate over the Democratic and Republican contenders. And her magic was still working in the primaries, where voters stayed at home in droves, following Andrea's advice that the stay-athomers turn out en masse for the November elections and give their vote to her as a write-in candidate.

Amazed pollsters found out that Andrea's strategy was working admirably. In primary elections to date, starting with Maine at the beginning of the year, voter turnout had been abysmally low. Apparently, the voters were saving themselves for Andrea, who had burst on the national scene like a neutron bomb. But if she did not destroy people and preserve porperty, worried observers saw her as a serious threat not only to the American political system but to American values as well. Her advocacy of free love, rat meat as a staple part of the nation's diet, and several other exotic ideas had fired the American imagination.

Rather than tailoring her speeches to fit regional audiences and special-interest groups, Andrea McKay provided the refreshing spectacle of saying the same thing to all people—instead of trying to be all things to all people—thereby avoiding the appearance of hypocrisy. Voters loved her, and stayed home at her bidding, and active, militant absenteeism hung like a poised dagger at the hopes of the Democratic and the Republican candidates alike. The best they could hope for from Andrea McKay's spoil-sport politics which siphoned votes away from both parties, the experts said, was that the election would be thrown into the House of Representatives, where the Democrats enjoyed a powerful majority.

The press of course played its part in Andrea's meteoric rise to political stardom. As October approached, Carlton was swamped by media personnel in such numbers that not even the natural truculence of the townspeople could drive them away. The town's favorite daughter had suddenly made Carlton famous, and there was a gradual, awkward warming up to the fact by its citizens. "Enjoy! Enjoy!" Joel Peters chortled in the *Chronicle*. Even tourists poured across the two bridges to eat greasy fried catfish and cornbread, to listen to the saga of Andrea McKay, to gawk at the old gray house down near the levee where it was said she grew up, and to stand on top of the massive levee to look down into the oily gray-green waters of the Mississippi where Andrea's father was said to have possibly committed suicide. Some of the more morbid visitors made pilgrimages to the cemetery where two graves side by side carried the names of Tom and Mary McKay on their tombstones; the third one, hardly larger than a big shoebox, carried only the inscription PATRICK, and his dates. This was said to be the final resting place of Andrea's love child, where some women tourists were photographed by the media as they wept bitter tears.

Andrea McKay was big news and big business, and Carlton could no longer keep the curious away. So there was a festive air about the town, even some bunting and a squeaky band for Columbus Day, with large posters of Andrea plastered on house walls. The high school—where Joel Peters's mother had taught, and which covertly trained SADIF agents in its night adult classes, in the absence of any children in Carlton; a fact which amazed many reporters—used its auditorium to house the press and its equipment during the day hours. At night, the townspeople filled the Carlton Hotel with their usual boisterousness. Justin himself functioned as a kind of unofficial press officer, pushed into the job by Joel Peters, and he arranged interviews with key townspeople, submitted himself to interviews about Andrea McKay and her background, and made himself quite useful with his own credentials from the *Washington Post* before the newspeople finally trickled away. But they would be back in November, they said, if Andrea was elected.

Justin had participated in all the excitement with a sense of detachment that did nothing to dull his natural keenness. While all America swooned over Andrea McKay and her quaint hometown, Justin saw Carlton as a lie, a farce, a movie set, and a staged production put together for buffoons. Nothing here was real except for one thing: a collective determination to give the impression that Carlton was really Andrea McKay's hometown and to hide the fact that it was a town of SADIF agents.

Thelma had said that the American people needed respectability and tragedy in Andrea McKay, mixed with just the right amount of scandal. And it was Carlton that gave them that; Justin's presence in Carlton gave it the necessary credibility. But the stories about Andrea McKay that America thrilled to—the death of her child and her parents, her tragic love affair, the details of her early life scattered like soiled toys across the panorama of the past to convince reporters that she indeed had existed here—impressed Justin as being just too transparent. Andrea and her town reminded him of the female agent he had killed in Paris—too real to be believed.

Except, of course, by people who needed to believe in something new every month or so. In that respect, Andrea McKay fit the bill admirably. As for the American people in this presidential year, Justin saw them as part of a declining civilization in its Age of Excrement. Far from showing themselves to be a nation of sheep, they appeared determined to distinguish themselves this coming November as a nation of dumb shits. But Americans as dumb shits had fallen into a kind of daze thrown around them by Andrea McKay. Made drunk and uncontrolled by the pervading smell of pure shit—packaged by SADIF, shoveled out by Andrea, with the CIA helpless to intervene—America indeed seemed to be a society consuming itself.

And then, in the very middle of October, several of the major polls showed that Andrea's ratings were slipping. SADIF was probably unaware of the American habit of turning instant celebrities into instant nobodies. In less than twenty-four hours, the trend had reversed itself; oversaturation had set in—the children had tired of the toy—and Andrea went from being frontrunner in the polls to lagging sadly behind.

The incumbent Republican president chose that moment to play his clever hole card. A small contingent of U.S. marines invaded the Central American nation of Nicaragua. There were several American casualties, and fighting was described as "fierce" by the press, which turned its attention almost entirely away from the coming elections and Andrea McKay. The Nicaraguan invasion was obviously a major mistake on the part of the Republican president; the communist world howled, along with every single one of America's so-called allies.

But the American people rallied around their president. His popularity in the polls rose like a hot-air balloon. The Democrátic candidate was jeered in Texas when he tried to rail against the invasion. Andrea McKay quickly and mysteriously dropped out of sight. And on October 17, two days after the Nicaraguan fighting broke out, Thelma Carew came to Justin in a near panic.

"Andrea's come back to Riverview," Thelma said. "My God, Justin! Is she really going to lose? What can we do?" She grabbed his hands in her own trembling ones. "My children's lives depend on Andrea's winning, Justin! I'm not with SADIF, or the KGB, or the CIA. I'm a woman, a mother, who is being forced to do these horrible things. Either I cooperate with them or they'll kill my children. Help me, Justin! Help me!"

She broke down altogether, and it was a wonderful moment for Justin Perry as he brought her into his arms to reassure her.

That same afternoon, the powerful antennae on Joel Peters's wooden house received a cryptic message from SADIF headquarters in Munich, Germany: ACTIVATE PHASE

FOUR. ACTIVATE PHASE FOUR. The message was intercepted by the CIA and passed along to the Old Man, who relayed it to Justin in Carlton.

Two hours later, at 4:25 P.M., Justin was physically attacked by Randy Whittaker, Fran's kid brother, in the Silver Dollar Bar in Carlton.

"You're making a whore out of my sister!" Randy screamed at Justin, and then swung.

Justin easily sidestepped, whopped the youth in the gut, and sat him down to sober up. "Take care of him, Jess," he said to the bartender, and tossed some bills on the bar. Then he went out. Everybody agreed that Justin had handled himself well with Randy Whittaker, that weird little cocksucker. As for Fran Whittaker, that little bitch hotel desk clerk, everybody knew about her. They'd all had a piece of that pie, they said.

SADIF's Phase Four was very effectively under way.

SIX

Justin went up the street to the Carlton Hotel, where he found Fran Whittaker waiting for him in his room. She didn't usually come to him so early, and especially not during the day. But she seemed surprised to find him in a foul mood.

"What's wrong, Justin?"

He dragged out his suitcase and his clothes as he told her. "I'm getting the hell out of Carlton," he growled. "I'm sick of this fucking dump! I'm sick of you! I'm sick of everything!"

Fran Whittaker paled. "Don't leave me, Justin. I don't know what I'd do." As though to tempt him, she unzipped her dress and stepped out of it into exquisite nakedness.

"You can always go back to fucking your kid brother," Justin said, with deliberate nastiness.

"Ah, Justin! Don't leave me!" She sounded stricken, dropping to her knees, kissing him passionately in the groin, her arms around his waist. He saw the tableau in the old-fashioned dresser mirror, and it excited him.

But he knocked her away with a slight cuff against her head. Looking up at him, her eyes glittered with pleasure.

"Don't go!" she hissed. "I'll do anything you want! I'll even tell you who killed Andrea's parents!"

Considering that Andrea had had no provable parents—Tom and Mary McKay had clearly proven to be fabrications of SADIF, along with everything else in this town—that would be a very formidable feat, Justin thought.

"You're just talking," he said cruelly. "You'd say anything to suck my dick, wouldn't you?"

She nodded in heated agreement. "Yes . . . yes . . . anything." She came across the floor to him on her knees.

He had his pants open, waiting for her. "Who killed Andrea's parents?" he said.

He stopped the forward thrust of her head a quarter of an inch away from him. Looking down on her, he felt a sense of incredible excitement.

She was with SADIF; one day he'd have to kill her as well. Perhaps he would kill her right now with his dick.

"Who killed them?" he said, taking it out.

Her eyes seemed to cross as she looked at its long, thick hardness curving toward her. "It was Randy, my brother! He killed them both!"

Snapping open the belt on his pants, he let them drop to his ankles, tightening the solid muscles in his legs and butt at the same time. Slowly, deliberately, he took off his shirt and pulled down his shorts, like a male whore stripping.

Her titties bounced provocatively as she crawled toward him, as though dedicated little animals did pushups in her chest. He reached out and caught her by the back of her head with both hands. Her eyes bulged as he pulled her to him.

With a heavy, eager groan, she took him greedily into her mouth. SADIF's Phase Four was still working, but the CIA's Phase Four was working as well. Her throat and jaws, even her very head in his hands, seemed to expand and contract as she sucked him. He watched the tableau in the mirror, and smiled.

*   *   *

Randy Whittaker's widely publicized confession to the murders of Andrea McKay's mother and father was unique in several respects. First, it came to the attention of the world on October 20, just two-and-a-half weeks before the national elections. Secondly, it carried the public's attention away from the administration's invasion of Nicaragua. And it placed Andrea McKay back in the national spotlight again. Her flagging performance on the popularity scale was enormously bolstered by the sordid scandal that exploded around her.

Out in Carlton, Illinois, the townspeople were reinvigorated and "agog," as Joel Peters reported in the *Chronicle*. "Murder most foul has been done," he wrote, in the manner of a minor Shakespeare, "and justice must be done. The people cry out for justice!"

If they did, Justin thought wryly as he folded the newspaper away, it was because they had been told to do so by SADIF, at least here in Carlton. He had to give SADIF grudging respect for its cleverness: the president had witlessly invaded Nicaragua, stealing Andrea's thunder; SADIF had counterattacked with the phony murders and Randy Whittaker's equally phony confession. As a result, Andrea was on the front pages and in the camera lights again.

But to exactly what limits was SADIF prepared to go to keep Andrea there? Justin wondered. With the elections only days away, it was now a no-holds-barred contest to see who would win this last stage of the battle for the public's mind—or, more aptly put, for the public's vote, since the conclusion that one vote equaled one mind had never seemed farther from the truth.

The public wanted scandal, intrigue, and melodrama in return for its ballot. Whoever paid the piper would get the disputed prize. In the final days of October, the incumbent president gave them twenty-five slaughtered marines, castrated and gutted by guerrillas in the jungles of Nicaragua. The outrage was seen on the six o'clock news, with a famous commentator describing the atrocities in solemn tones to arouse voter indignation.

But Andrea's camp fought back with a lurid confession by Randy Whittaker. "I killed Mary McKay because I loved her, and she wouldn't go away with me. I knew that she was older than me, almost old enough to be my mother. But I loved her nevertheless. She is the only woman I have ever loved. As for Tom McKay, he had a crush on me and couldn't keep his hands off of me. I killed him to make him leave me alone."

What Randy really said, in the latter respect, was: "He was a fag, the sonofabitch. He used to suck me off while I flexed." And what about his sister, Fran, who had turned him in to the police? "What about my sister? Do I feel bad because she turned me in? Well, who wouldn't feel bad? We'd been lovers ever since she was fourteen and I was twelve. You'd think that she'd show some loyalty after all that time."

Then, Andrea went on national television, dressed in deep black, looking stricken but brave. Justin saw the broadcast on the set in the hotel lobby. The place was jammed with locals who gave the appearance of being anxious to forgive Andrea. All she had to do was to say the right words. The scandal that touched her by indirection could give her the majority vote, or take it away from her altogether. The sense of waiting expectation in Carlton, Justin knew, was being repeated in front of television sets all over America.

Could she pull it off?

"Randy Whittaker has sent me a telegram asking for my forgiveness," she began, in the whispery voice of the newly bereaved. "And I would like to take this opportunity not only to forgive Randy for his deeds but to thank each and every one of you in the television audience for the wonderful show of support you have given me in these tragic days.

"But who am I to forgive Randy Whittaker when I have sinned so dreadfully myself? There is no need for me to go into my own transgressions; they have been amply and truthfully revealed by our great American press. It is not for me to forgive, but to beg the forgiveness of each and every one of you. And if I am by God's will elected to this great office to which I aspire as the just penance for my deeds, then I solemnly swear that I shall spend the rest of my life trying to undo the evil that I have wrought, the evil that has touched me, and the evil that has touched each and every one of you because of me."

She pulled it off. *If I am elected to this great office to which I aspire as the just penance for my deeds.* She had made the American presidency a penance; and she would win. Justin suspected that his eyes were the only dry ones in the Carlton hotel. And he suspected that other eyes were dripping all over America, in a kind of emotional gonorrhea brought about by the inspired maudlinness of Andrea McKay.

But, however maudlin—and that was what was wanted anyway: the public indeed wanted to forgive and to get its jollies by feeling morally superior in the act of forgiving—Andrea's performance knocked the Nicaraguan slaughter off of prime-time television and the nation's front pages and put her back in the driver's seat again.

If all went well in the next few days, Justin considered, she would knock the president out of the White House as well, and replace him as SADIF's first chief executive of any nation anywhere, ever. Only one thing remained to be done: to maintain its advantage, SADIF and the FLP, its political arm, had to make sure that the drums of false piety kept beating over Randy Whittaker.

His was the sin that besmirched them all; Andrea's sin was that she and her parents had been sinners. Only the public's forgiveness would take away the staircase of sins that spiraled over Andrea's bowed head; Andrea had said so on television. And the public had been transformed by Andrea into Jesus Christ, the Lamb of God that taketh away the sins of the world, at least this corner of it.

Even a less vain and empty audience than the American one could have been forgiven for feeling just a little puffed up after all of that. Still, it was essential for SADIF to maintain its emotional advantage. For starters, the unrevised version of Randy's confession was leaked to the press. Full of profanity, incest, homosexual intrigue, thwarted love, sizzling hate, adultery, and finally murder, it oozed out around the American public and they licked it up like cream.

And yet, not one single word of it was true.

There had been no parents for Randy Whittaker to murder. "Andrea McKay" was a Russian madwoman trained for years in English and Americanisms by Thelma Carew in Moscow. The real Andrea McKay, she of that long-ago summer sacrifice, had been blown up along with the pumpkins on the Illinois state highway nearly a year ago, so that the phony Andrea could appropriate her name if not her history.

"I was the one that suggested Betty's background," Thelma told Justin. "But then, we had to discard the whole thing. Betty was just too young and had too many real contacts in the States that the phony Betty—Andrea McKay—would have to convince. So we decided just to use her name. But by that time, the order to get rid of Betty—the *real* Andrea McKay, the one you knew in Orlando—had already gone out from Moscow, and it was too late to stop it."

A monumental scheme, sometimes awkward, sometimes

brilliant, for placing the phony Andrea McKay in the White House. A plot hatched by SADIF and the KGB. Carlton was SADIF's contribution to the joint operation; a town founded nearly thirty years ago in the heart of America, to train SADIF agents and send them out into the world for conquest, terrorism, and just plain mischief. And while they were still in Carlton, an arrogant exercise in roleplaying and deception in the comparative isolation of the Mississippi island enclave.

"They needed you here," Thelma explained, "to give believability to the place once outsiders came pouring in, especially the press. You'd keep some eager reporter from going too deep. From digging up those phony graves in the cemetery, for example. Or really going down deep and checking birth records, things like that. Everything about Andrea is phony, from her name, her background, her records. Even her nationality. She is a Russian, a former actress who went mad. The role was perfect for her, partly because of her own talents and partly because of the American need for a mad president; it would fulfill our favorite fantasy, our most horrible expectations."

Thelma had been carefully selected for her part in the operation. She had been romanced at the University of Florida by the KGB agent, had gone to Russia and married him, and had even been led into childbirth so that the children could be held hostage as a guarantee to her loyal participation. Then, the KGB allegedly getting wind of the SADIF scheme and leaking just enough of it to the CIA to ensure a *lack* of CIA participation, for fear of stampeding the voters into Andrea's corner as a rebellion against the U. S. intelligence apparatus.

This was Operation Orlando from the other side of the fence. The so-called loan of Thelma Carew to the CIA as liaison between the Russian and American agencies had given SADIF a wider area to work inside of. A special and costly operation, but with a prize certainly worth the effort and the waiting for: nothing less than to wreck the political apparatus of the United States and to put a combination SADIF-KGB agent into the White House, if the plan were successful. And if it failed at any point along the way, the entire U.S. intelligence system, indeed, the U.S. society itself, would be made to look like a bunch of asses.

"I knew all the time what was going on," Thelma said. "I felt awful, almost insane myself sometimes. Poor Aunt Eugenia—they poisoned her to provoke you into going public with the whole scheme. They had nothing to lose either way. The more the CIA kept quiet, the more they pushed toward the final objective—the presidency. I was terrified that the plan would succeed, and terrified that it wouldn't. But if it does fail, then my children will die, whether I'm responsible for the failure or not.

"Still, something in me rebelled. I kept trying to let you know, to put you off the false track and onto the right one, without coming out and telling you. That's why I invented the story about Betty's baby. I knew that you hadn't ejaculated in her that night. Betty told me so herself, and she didn't have any sex that summer with anyone else. Then the apparent mixup about whether Andrea's—Betty's—parents were mad or not. Betty's parents did die in a madhouse, but Andrea McKay's were not mad.

"This Betty—Andrea McKay—*is* mad. All I told you about that is true. I'm assigned to her at all times when she's at Riverview. Dr. Porter is with her in her travels. She does sometimes go wild and manage to escape, but that is usually because she wants to have sex. Dr. Porter, who is her chief male contact, is hopelessly homosexual. She goes out to have sex, and then she comes back to us when she's satisfied. That's what she was out doing when SADIF panicked last November and thought that she'd get caught. That's when they raided all those madhouses, hoping that Andrea would be lost in the crowd. And she was. Dr. Porter's job, and mine, is to make sure that she has her drug at specific times. Without it, she does go completely mad.''

On this side of the fence that was Operation Orlando, the CIA's side, Justin Perry had played primarily a waiting game at the Old Man's orders. He had been interned in the asylum primarily to convince SADIF that the CIA was in the dark and searching for leads and, at the same time, to push SADIF into activating Andrea. After that, he had spent nearly this entire year in Carlton, lending authenticity to the myth that was Carlton, and the authenticity that SADIF wanted, or the exposure of the scheme that SADIF would gloat over.

At the same time, Justin and the CIA had worked feverishly to bring about the oversaturation in the press that had caused her ratings to slip. Justin had written articles about her and passed along information to the CIA's propaganda department, which was written up and fed to the press. Good news or bad, it was planted in newspapers and magazines all over the country. The CIA also paid radio and television stations to put Andrea on shows. And when the national press had arrived in Carlton, Justin had functioned as briefing officer, steering the more eager correspondents away from possible dangerous areas in the saga of Andrea McKay, probably to the great amusement of SADIF, which wanted a mad female president but would have easily settled for a juicy scandal showing up the American gullibility.

Bob Dante has put in his appearance on the island disguised as Dr. Eric Lindstrom, the blond ecologist, actually inspecting the island for the best site for the emplacement of hundreds of tons of TNT when it should be time to blow the place sky high. The explosives had been placed at strategic positions around the island when the cargo freighter had been deliberately grounded. CIA divers had done the job with the explosives while the freighter was being floated. Bob Dante had placed the TNT, but Justin Perry would push the detonator—if things came to that.

Now, with Orlando's Phase Four actively under way— accurately matching that of SADIF's—the attention getter of Randy Whittaker's "confession" to the murder of Andrea's "parents," SADIF was playing the incident for all it was worth, with the CIA acquiescence and Justin's hearty participation. And always the Old Man's warning not very far in the back of Justin's mind: *Play it very cool, Justin. SADIF needs us. They're trying desperately to get us to come out of the closet, fighting mad, and to tell everything. But for their own purposes. We're trying desperately to stay in the closet, for our own purposes. We certainly can't afford to make a martyr out of Andrea McKay, however mad and phony she might be.*

"It sounds like two teams of fags fighting," Justin said dryly. But he knew what the Old Man meant; martyrdom for Andrea meant either the presidency for her, or a scandal inside the American government that would rock it to its very foundations. As it happened, the American public, in its own gullible way, had cooperated quite effectively with the enemy's plans.

After Justin filled Thelma in, she held her head in her hands. "It's so confusing . . . almost maddening. And my children, Justin. What am I to do?"

He caught her in his arms and kissed her, trying to pour strength from his body into hers. "Do this," he said, and he told her.

The night following Andrea McKay's brilliant appearance on television, in which she agreed to accept the White House as a form of penance, Thelma brought her to Carlton. It was not a part of the script, perhaps not even necessary. But Justin was consumed by curiosity to see this woman in person. And this time—not like in the asylum, when he had been drugged—this time with all of his senses and his peter intact.

"She's down at the levee," Thelma said. "And I have not given her the injection." She hesitated, her eyes wide and frightened. "They wouldn't let her come alone. There are four men."

"Good," Justin said, and his grin was terrible as he slipped into his shoulder holster carrying the .38. Then he went out whistling. It had been months since he'd killed anybody.

He had the first feeling that something was wrong when he saw the isolation at the levee. Normally, at this hour—it was nearly ten o'clock—there were motorcycle riders, beer drinkers, strollers, lovers, and kibitzers on the broad green mall approaching the levee. Especially on a balmy night like this one, with the full moon pouring down like liquid silver.

A killer's moon, Justin thought impassionately. His every sense was alive. He had gone down to the levee in a black commando suit, the .38 holstered at his shoulder, a twelve-inch, razor-sharp bayonet strapped to his calf. The woods grew almost down to the levee and the mall—large, squat oaks and tall, thick pines, that Justin used to his advantage. A killer's moon, a hunter's moon; he felt the blood of hunting and killing pumping in his veins. And there was a warmth in his groin, like a fever. He saw the grayish-white gulls cutting over the Mississippi; their cries were sharp and sudden, as though they had been startled from sleep by nightmares involving humans. The river slapped up against the levee wall like the sloshing of wet thighs.

He saw the first man just ahead of him in the woods; leaning back, he was pissing in the wind like a little

Danish boy. Justin waited until he was finished, standing right behind him. When he heard the man's zipper being pulled up, he wrapped his arm around the man's thick neck, almost lovingly, choking off his cry, and rammed the bayonet hard through the ribs, stabbing the heart from the back. The man slumped to the ground, making a small whimpering noise like an injured dog.

"Henry? That you, Henry?"

The voice came from some ten feet away. Justin saw the other man as he stepped out into a patch of moonlight in the polka-dot woods, a can of beer in one hand, a gun in the other. Justin stepped quickly, silently, behind a concealing oak. Waiting, he remembered that trees had been sacred to the goddess Ceres in mythology; it was she who had cursed Erisichthon with an insatiable hunger, after he'd offended her by cutting down an oak tree, until Erisichthon had finally consumed himself.

Justin's bayonet bit into the man's heart as he passed; beer flew from the can as his hand flew up. Justin ripped the gun from his other hand at the same time. The safety was still on.

The other two men were standing together near the edge of the woods, talking softly. "You think he'll show up?" one said. The other one nodded. "He'll be here." He was young, standing halfway in the moonlight, dressed up as though he'd been snatched from a date with his best girl to take on this assignment.

Bending, Justin picked up a rock and threw it to the right. The young man turned, reaching for his gun. He still had it in his holster, he was that young. Justin dived, bringing him to the ground. Then, lifting him lightly as he flipped backward with the boy's body as a shield, he felt the boy's body tense and then give as a slug from the other man's gun bit into him.

Justin was glad he hadn't killed the boy. But even as he

thought it, he had sent the bayonet winging through the air with a practiced flick of his wrist. The fourth man caught it in the neck, and went down making ugly, gurgling sounds. Justin pulled out the bayonet, wiped it on the man's nylon jacket, and then proceeded to the levee.

He saw Andrea McKay standing on the levee's top. Tall, slender, she wore a brilliant white dress that gave her a ghostly look in the moonlight. Moving in a low crouch, Justin went up the steps to the flat top of the levee. Below him, seventy-five feet down on the water side, he saw the river break sluggishly against the sloping barrier, then shudder away in white foam.

The woman had her back turned to him when he spoke in fluent Russian. "What is your name?" he said.

"Nadia Mendelyeev," the woman said calmly as she turned. Her face was very white in contrast to the mane of black hair, blowing in the wind like a mass of serpents. He could even see the slanting green eyes, as sly as a cat's.

Then her ripe, red lips broke into a knowing smile. "So you have come," she said, also in Russian. "And you are very clever, Mr. Perry. I shall see to it that Dr. Carew is severely punished for her indiscretion."

"She told me nothing," Justin said. Although trying to protect Thelma or her children was a moot point now. Very little could be done for her children if the Russians really wanted them dead. As for the dead men down in the woods, that also made very little difference now. Operation Orlando, on both sides, had moved into a kind of no-man's-land, an area of hesitation where either side could strike out with comparative impunity against the other from now until the elections. It was like a team horsing around in the locker room until game time; the trophy was the presidency, and the final decision rested in the hands of the voters.

He breathed deeply, taking another few tentative steps

towards the woman. A killer's moon, filtering down on them now like a benign mist, made her green eyes glitter. His heart thundered; his loins burned. He desperately wanted to fuck. Killing always affected him that way. His dick stiffened against the tight-fitting commando suit; made of lightweight nylon—he was naked underneath—it slid against his dick and thighs as though it was the woman's hands.

She was also coming toward him. She was immensely beautiful, far more so than he would have thought from seeing her on television. But her beauty was mature, certainly the result of suffering and intrigue; he had the idea that she must have been a great actress before madness had laid her low. Her walk, the outward thrust of her pelvis clearly seen through the thin white material, the floodlight effect from the misting moon, gave the whole scene a sense of studied theatricality.

He felt a kind of subtle change in the woman as she closed in on him. Her bare arms and throat were marble white; the long white garment whipped backward from the wind, showing the curvaceous imprint of her body, the slight rise of her sex. She might have been a ship's figurehead come to life—ornamental, pulsating, fiercely tantalizing. Her hands went to his groin, felt, grabbed, squeezed, clawed, and slithered away, satisfied. She smelled of gin and perfume, subtly mixed. Her hair, blowing in the wind, reached out and swept his face.

"I had your child," she said. "It died." She turned her head away. "I have loved you ever since."

Thelma had taught her those words, but they seemed to be the dialogue from some old play. Just how long had it been since she'd last taken her controlling drug? It would have been difficult to think of her as mad if he had not known that she was. He decided to go along with her act. And his dick was massively hard as he remembered that other moonlit night in his cell at Riverview.

"I have loved you too," he said, standing very close to her, arms around her loveliness, grinding his hardness up into her.

"You have?" Her long white neck swiveled, her head came up. Her black hair swept back, carried in the hands of the wind. He felt the levee thunder under his feet as the waves below broke against the wall in a long line of white sperm. Her face was smooth and classic in its beauty, a Nereid's masque. "Why have you not come to me, then? Why have you let me suffer?"

It was hard to believe that she was Russian; her English was too perfect. He lapsed into Russian. "They would not let me come to you," he said.

"They sometimes do that," she said sadly. Her eyes burned like hot emeralds. She also spoke in Russian, and seemed not to have noticed the shift. He felt a mounting *something* in her, and wondered if her madness was about to spill over.

It was. Her hands went to her breasts and touched a zipper, then brought it down to her knees, stooping in a graceful, almost girlish way as she stepped naked out of the white garment.

Against his will, he sucked in his breath. She was white, beautiful, exquisite. He felt mad himself as he quickly undressed. The wind whipped around him like a soft garment of many tongues. The two of them stood alone on the high levee, a naked god and his goddess bathed in the song of the moon that only the two of them could hear.

He dropped to his knees before her, holding her by her high pelvis, and lapped between her legs until she opened them to his tongue. He savored the salty sweetness hidden in the bush of tight hair, felt all of her nerve ends converge on the probing tip of his tongue. She stiffened and fell backward, a ballerina in the hands and hot mouth of her *danseur*. His teeth slashed her, and she shuddered; he had a compulsion to eat her up.

She was lying flat on the levee. He slid up her body and sought her lips, his dick resting between the hollow of her legs; he felt the swollen head of it hit against the cement as she tightened the muscles of her thighs around it. As he kissed her, something sweet and maddening filtered into his mouth like forbidden liquor.

''Andrea . . . Andrea McKay,'' he said, down into the delicate curve of her neck. He was as close to love and insanity as he'd ever been. He left her mouth and went back between her legs again—sucking, chewing, gnawing—as his penis slid in and out of her mouth like a giant piston. He shuddered as she shuddered, the sperm shooting out of him like a thin hot rope down her throat.

Then he turned, lifted her legs slightly, and entered her. She screamed and clawed at his back, fighting away. But he followed her relentlessly, ramming. He caught her shoulders and held her; he could feel the trembling in her legs around his waist. His balls slapped like bell clappers against her ass, hurting him; but the pain felt good.

He thrusted with uncontrolled passion as the gulls screamed around them. He had never known such violence, such pleasure, such awful, aching, sweet pain with a woman. He could have fucked her forever. The river thundered against the levee with heightened fury, as though protesting Justin's violence.

Andrea McKay was completely mad when he withdrew from her. He felt completely mad himself, as though she had somehow tainted him. His dick was wet with blood, as though he had fucked a virgin.

It was with some difficulty that he got Andrea back into her clothes and into Thelma's car that he had parked on the other side of the woods near the levee. She had been violent at first, but with surprising moments of lucidity, as Thelma had said.

"So you have found me out," she ranted in Russian, flinging her arms about like white snakes. "But it is too late now. I will be elected president, thanks to your stupid American public. And it will not serve to kill me now, as you very well know. We will have another of our candidates in your next election . . . and the next . . . and the next. . . . My death now would be a beginning rather than an ending."

He wished she would shut the fuck up, because it was all too true. She sounded like Nikita Khrushchev, spitting out Russian, weaving and writhing in front of him like impassioned strains of Slavic music.

Then she was calm again. "I love you," she said. "You are the first man ever to make me feel like a woman, to feel the *violence* of being woman. I'll never forget you." And she went to her knees to suck him, gnawing at him through the suit. He wanted her again, but he brought her to her feet. "I'll never forget you either," he said. And he meant it; he really meant it.

Then she fell into a kind of comatose state that held her silent and almost stiff, like a department store mannequin, until Justin turned her over to Thelma. "Take her back to Riverview," he said. "But give her the injection now."

He watched as Thelma prepared and administered the shot from her satchel. "Are you convinced now that I told you the truth?" she said. Her voice was charged with bitterness. "Now they really will kill my children."

He was too hyped up to care. "I'm convinced. Now get the hell out of here. I'll get the Old Man to do whatever he can for your kids."

"Thank you," she said. But her voice was still hard. She's jealous, Justin thought. It made him grin, unbend some. He kissed her hard, holding himself back from fucking her. She had to get Andrea back to Riverview.

But he did take her hand and smoothed it down the swollen front of his commando suit, curling her fingers around the hardness there. "Come back in two or three hours," he said. "I'll be waiting in the hotel."

She melted completely. "I'll be here," she said. "Wild horses couldn't keep me away."

But SADIF might, he thought grimly as she pulled off. Andrea McKay sat stiffly beside her in the front seat. Suddenly the moon slid behind a stray cloud and the night took on a more grotesque cast.

And Justin Perry wanted to kill more.

The murders at the levee and the sex with Andrea McKay had heated him. Some instinct told him that there were victims in the woods, and he went there. And saw about a dozen townspeople of Carlton, all of them SADIF, lynch Fran Whittaker and her brother Randy.

SADIF was sacrificing two of its agents to maintain its infernal advantage in the press over the dead in Nicaragua. It had always been a contest between SADIF and the incumbent president, Justin thought, as he crouched behind a giant oak to watch. The Democratic contender had never really been in the running because he lacked the means to pull off great stunts that called for forgiveness.

Fran and Randy Whittaker died well in the name of SADIF, hauled up to the oak branch by hefty men. Tomorrow's media reports would carry sanctimonious stories about the outraged people of Carlton who could not bear evil in their midst, how they had broken Randy out of jail to lynch him, and lynched the incestuous sister as well. It was a gory sight—the two bodies being strangled at the ends of ropes like pitiful dolls—but not a satisfying one. In his present mood, Justin felt cheated.

Were there no clean hands in Carlton? He was aware that the Bible had God asking the same question before deciding on Noah. Filled with murder himself, Justin felt a need for salvation, if not his own, then someone else's. The struggling bodies in the nooses did not give him satisfaction. He felt that the lynchers of Carlton had strayed over into his own domain. Wasn't he the Assassin? If he had killed Fran and Randy, he would have killed them kinder; murder of that sort ought not to be left to amateurs.

He turned away and crept like a lean beast to the home of Joel Peters and his mother. The human part of him needed at least a symbolic good, someone to build an ark for. Could he find it in Joel Peters? As much as he'd disliked the fat little man, he'd felt an affinity for him from the first day. They both had shared traumas about mothers. Certainly Mrs. Peters's soul had not been compromised; even SADIF could not pierce the armor of her bad manners and her cantankerousness.

He was aware that his mind was running loose. But it was a thing that he sometimes let happen when he was in the middle of murder. How did a totally sane man stand up and say, *I am a killer*, and justify it by any of the existing moral standards? No, the best thing to do was to let his mind hang loose from time to time; the justification would present itself in the breach.

Also, events of the past year suddenly seemed to accumulate and explode their bile around his head. Salvation, redemption, symbolic good—he wondered if Andrea had passed her madness on to him after all—were expressions that belonged more properly in the vocabulary of a preacher than in the thoughts of a killer like himself. Or was he only trying to justify the burning appetite he felt for death?

He found Joel in his living room, typing up a lead article about the lynching for tomorrow's weekly edition of the *Chronicle*. The event had been timed to help Joel sell papers and to get Andrea into the White House. There were no clean hands in Carlton after all. He felt like a kid who has just found out that Santa Claus is a fake. Perhaps God had felt the same way before He'd unleashed the flood.

Joel Peters had let Justin in cordially. He seemed to ignore the .38 in Justin's hand. Indeed, he also seemed to be in a kind of euphoria. The sense of madness expanded in Justin, like a rubber band being stretched. Joel Peters wore pink bedroom slippers, pink silk pajamas underneath a checkered smoking jacket.

"Mother gave them to me last Christmas," he said, by way of explanation. "She got one of the church women to wheel her over to the department store. It was very painful for her." He arranged a chair for Justin facing the mother's bedroom door. "I couldn't *not* wear them; she's very sensitive, you know."

Justin suddenly felt very tired and flopped in the chair. He wondered if Mrs. Peters had also bought the lipstick and powder that Joel wore. "Did you arrange the lynching, Joel?"

His red lips split in a big smile, showing very large teeth. His eyes twinkled behind his glasses. "*I* arrange it? Goodness, no! The respectable people of this town took the prisoners from jail, afrer overpowering the guards. It says so right here in my article. Why on earth do you think that *I'd* arrange such a thing?"

"Because you're SADIF, Joel. The whole fucking town is SADIF."

Joel seemed very amused, a fat fag in his lipstick and his pink slippers and pajamas. "Who do you think would believe such a thing, Justin? You're excited. And tired. I can see it in your face. Wouldn't . . . wouldn't you like for me to suck you off, or something? It certainly would relax you."

He felt no disgust; only a profound pity. "No, I would not like for you to suck me off, Joel. I came here to kill you."

That seemed to tickle him even more. "Dear, dear! Are you aware that you and I have the same initials; Justin Perry, Joel Peters? I used to dabble in astrology, and that means something important, although I've forgotten exactly what. And why would you want to kill me?"

"Because you're SADIF, Joel, and we don't take prisoners. Is your mother also in the organization? We know about the shortwave set down in the basement, Joel. We've been monitoring your messages since long before I got here. We know that Carlton is all SADIF. But what about your mother?" He knew that he was making a big mistake, like Dionysus with his lantern looking for one honest man. "Is she SADIF, Joel?"

The bedroom door burst open like an explosion. And the mother *stood* there with a double-barrel shotgun in her hand and the wrath of God twisting her face. "You dirty sonofabitch!" she screamed. "Of course I'm SADIF! And proud of it! And one day, we will rule the world!" She swung the shotgun up.

Justin reacted automatically. He slammed sideways out of the chair, bringing the .38 up at the same time. He heard the shotgun blast as the wicker-backed chair shattered into pieces. Some of the splinter struck Justin. He pulled the trigger of the .38 and saw the old woman stagger backward. He had got her squarely in the center of her forehead. Her mouth dropped open, and then she died. Her nightgown was the same color pink as Joel's ensemble.

Joel hadn't moved through all of this. Indeed, his fat fingers were still poised over the typewriter keys. Only his nose seemed to wrinkle, like a fat rabbit's, irritated by the unholy smell of gunpowder. "I told her it was a mistake," he said. His voice was toneless, without color or emotion.

"She was our leader, but she didn't always make the right decision." He got up from the chair with a sigh, arranging his pajamas across his behind. Justin watched him closely, the .38 aimed and waiting. "I suppose you're going to kill me too?"

"Yes, Joel. It's better this way. We don't take prisoners. There're just too many of you."

Joel nodded. "Yes. I suppose you're right." Suddenly his face twisted in a spasm of emotion. "God, I've always hated myself! Please make it quick!"

He closed his eyes, folding his hands in a tight fist against his chest. And Justin shot him through the heart.

Justin went back to the hotel and packed his bag. The town was semideserted, with most of the militants out in the woods enjoying the lynching. Then he drove Joel Peters's blue Ford LTD out of Carlton and met Thelma on the highway driving back from Riverview.

"Let's go to Chicago," he said. "Carlton's not safe anymore."

She looked at him closely as he slid in beside her. "Are you safe?" she said.

It was an ambiguous question—"Is it safe for me to be with you now?" she was really saying—and it irritated him. It was as though she had smelled his madness before. "Yes, I'm safe," he said. Although it was true that he hadn't been especially safe before.

"How's Andrea doing?" he asked. He took her hand and laid it on his dick.

"Being presidential," Thelma said coldly, although her fingers curled around him, savoring the hardness. "She also complained of pain in her sex area. I gave her Valium."

Justin grinned and aimed the car out into the stark moonlight.

Somewhere between Carlton and Chicago, he stopped and made love to Thelma with great tenderness, perhaps as a penance for the violence he'd done to Andrea McKay and to all other women. Perhaps even as a penance for the fact that in the last moments after the bullet struck Mrs. Peters, before she toppled to the floor, he'd felt a sense of incredible exhilaration and release.

As though he'd finally rid himself of Anna Mason, the woman he had thought was his real mother. *God, I've always hated myself!* Joel Peters's heartfelt cry might have been Justin Perry's, if his false mother had had her way with him. . . . He shot his cum into Thelma . . . and wished it had been Andrea McKay moaning underneath his weight. Still, he had a very real sense of having cleared up old accounts; Anna Mason would never haunt him again.

Justin left the car in Chicago and flew out to Washington with Thelma within the hour. The Old Man had summoned them all to CIA headquarters for urgent consultations. Election day was only three days away, and Andrea McKay still held a commanding lead in the polls over both the Democratic and the Republican candidates. And that lead would go up as soon as America found out about the lynchings in Carlton, giving the public a chance to forgive Andrea for having come from such a place. The incumbent Republican president continued his carnage in Nicaragua without asking for forgiveness. Indeed, he made it very much appear as though the fault for his invasion of Nicaragua lay with Russia, and with certain elements of the American people, an observation for which the public would never forgive him.

Meanwhile, Andrea McKay was riding high. When asked about her own lack of a vice-presidential running mate, she laughed and said, "I'll pick one of the losing candidates for that job." Her arrogance was thought to be a cute joke all over America; it was also thought by seventy-three percent of the voting public that she would win the election. America's leading newspapers, including the *Washington*

Post and the *New York Times*, came out in her favor. Nothing short of a miracle could keep Andrea McKay out of the White House.

Early in the evening of election day, Justin Perry and Bob Dante went to the steambath to await the results.

Dante kept returning to the subject of destroying Carlton, like a dog to a buried bone. "I don't see why it has to be destroyed," he said, with surprising petulance. "It's an island; we could ring it in with troops and leave it at that. They could grow their own food, and take care of themselves."

It did not surprise Justin that Dante thought as he did— Justin himself had more than a few qualms about blowing up twelve thousand people—but that Dante kept bringing it up. The question was essentially a moral one; Operation Orlando, it seemed, had opened that particular part of Pandora's box more than any other.

"You only planted the dynamite, Bob. I'm the one who has to push the plunger."

They had left the big-breasted whores and were soaking away the remnants of sex inside the steam room. The baths were a CIA hangout, and they could talk with relative impunity. But the steam room was empty except for the two of them.

"But it's something you want to do, isn't it?" Dante said.

"Yes," Justin said quietly, turning away. "It's something I want to do, Bob."

How could he explain what he felt to his friend? It pissed him off that he even had to. Anyway, the decision was the Old Man's to make. But Justin was far too honest to hide behind the blind that he was just following orders. He wanted to destroy Carlton for reasons that had nothing to do with following orders.

The Sons and Daughters in Freedom, as an international terrorist organization with unlimited funds and fanatically dedicated manpower, represented a very real threat to the safety and sanity of the world. It was, in truth, an empire of evil—far more so than Russia was—because it came from no single country, followed no single creed. Independent and opportunistic, it took advantage of any and every occasion to cause death, confusion, and disorder.

Take Operation Orlando, for example. America and Russia were clear-cut adversaries, each dedicated to its own individual ideology, however wrongheaded each might be. Russia's participation in Operation Orlando was designed, ultimately, to serve its own national ends; SADIF's participation was designed to bring America to her knees. America was SADIF's main target; tomorrow, the world would follow.

If Russia could be said to be an honorable enemy— honorable in the sense that it at least wanted to preserve one small communist corner of the world for itself, after all others were swept away—then SADIF was a powerful, important, and irresponsible mischief maker: it threw the dice blindly and tried to capitalize on any numbers that came up. Win, lose, or draw it was all the same to SADIF, which was dedicated to destroying nations in the name of its own organization.

The present attack on the American political system was SADIF's boldest gamble to date. And Carlton, Illinois— that fabricated town crawling with SADIF agents in the heart of America—was SADIF's most arrogant incursion ever into the American consciousness. In the same way that the nation would become a laughingstock before the world if Operation Orlando were ever found out and whether Andrea McKay won the presidency or not—the fact that she had got within shouting distance of the White House would be as big an embarrassment if it was ever found

170

out—Carlton was an occasion for snickers and finger point-ing at the vulnerability and chilling stupidity of the greatest power on earth.

In that respect, neither the press, nor the government, nor even the American people were at fault. SADIF the archvillian was omnipresent and pure evil; in another day and age, it would have been called Satan. Even Russia was not invulnerable to its power, as Operation Orlando clearly demonstrated. SADIF had put the project together and then deliberately called the Soviet Union's attention to the fact. And Russia had fallen headlong into the trap, even provid-ing that part of the apparatus that had to do with Andrea McKay, and Thelma Carew, and Thelma's children.

No nation or individual would be safe from such machi-nations as long as SADIF survived. Carlton was fine evi-dence of its power that had to be destroyed, with the muddy waters of the Mississippi washing over the face of the island, to leave no trace that a mocking, smirking nest of rats had ever existed there. And America must be ever alert that its freedom did not give license to terror breeding in its own midst, evil masquerading as good.

Damn it! Didn't Dante understand that? What the fuck was wrong with him anyway?

They were soaping themselves down in the shower room when Dante told him. "I fell in love, Justin. A beautiful girl I met there when I was planting the TNT."

Justin nodded, feeling his chest tighten. "You didn't tell her anything, did you, Bob?"

"No. I'm not quite that stupid." He laughed bitterly. "She seemed to be the nicest girl I've ever met in my life, Justin. She wouldn't let me even kiss her. She told me she was in love with someone else. She worked at the hotel in Carlton. A real fine girl, Justin. Her name was Fran Whittaker. You would have liked her yourself."

Justin reached out and touched his friend's shoulder. "I

171

did like her, Bob. But she's dead now. Haven't you read the papers?''

"No. I've been too busy studying assignment sheets." He searched Justin's eyes, seeing the truth there. "Did you kill her, Justin?"

"I didn't kill her, Bob." He was very gentle; he'd had some very close brushes with love himself. "But she was SADIF, Bob. Definitely SADIF. She gave her life for the organization." He didn't really believe that—her life had been taken by the organization, hers and her brother Randy's— but it seemed to have a heroic sound about it that might appeal to Dante.

"I loved her," Dante said.

Justin took a deep breath. "So did I, Bob. Many times. I lived in the hotel there, you know."

Dante dropped his soap and swung. But Justin caught him easily by the wrist.

"Easy, Bob."

They locked eyes, standing naked in the showers. Then Dante pulled his wrist away. "I'm sorry, Justin. I guess I've been a fool. Blow the fucking place up."

"It's not really decided," Justin said.

But it had been decided; Justin wanted to spare his friend that.

Dante seemed his usual self as they dressed and went out to the restaurant in the baths. They were finishing up thick steaks when Justin was called to the telephone. It was only a few minutes before he came back.

"Andrea McKay's been elected president by a very wide margin," he told Dante. "Also, Andrea has got away from Dr. Porter. She's running around naked on her way back to Carlton. She apparently thinks I'm still there."

Dante wiped his mouth and got to his feet. "What's my job, Justin?" All business now, he slapped Justin's shoulder and grinned. "And I'm sorry about that scene in the shower. You should have slugged me. What does the Old Man want me to do?''

"Thelma's children were snatched from the KGB and have been successfully smuggled out of Moscow," Justin said. "They got them out in mailbags on the embassy plane. Now they're under heavy guard at our embassy in London. The Old Man wants you to pick them up."

"Will do," Dante said. "And how about you?"

Justin's face turned grim; he couldn't lie to his friend now. "I'm going out to Carlton. I'm to stuff Andrea back onto the island and then blow the whole fucking thing up."

Dante showed no apparent emotion. They paid their bills and were driven to Dulles Airport where two supersonic jets were warmed up and waiting for them. One would take Dante to London; the other would carry Justin to Chicago, then a fast helicopter ride out to the fields between Riverview and Carlton.

Where Andrea McKay was being chased through the moonstruck night by dogs, sheriff's deputies, and newspaper reporters, who knew only that a naked madwoman had broken out of Riverview Sanatarium. But they did not know that she was Andrea McKay, president-elect of the United States. Justin's job was to get to her and to kill her before any of them did find out.

EPILOGUE

Two months later, Justin Perry sat in the quiet, tropical gardens of the Marymount Sanatarium outside of Ocho Rios in Jamaica. It was January now, but while most of the United States and western Europe reeled under the icy effects of the worst winter in a hundred years, Jamaica was warm and tranquil. A gentle breeze lifted from the shimmering blue ocean far below, bringing with it the flavor of salt and sun as it reached the mountaintop where the sanatarium sat.

Watching the other patients coming and going—some in wheelchairs pushed by white-uniformed orderlies, others who were ambulatory, attended by nurses or relatives—Justin felt content and perfectly relaxed as his mind went back to that moonlit night in Illinois two months ago when he'd gone out in the helicopter from Chicago to intercept Andrea McKay.

They spotted her from the air, only a few miles away from the bridge that crossed the river into Carlton. The pilot, a lanky, good-looking black air-force lieutenant, set the unmarked chopper down in an old wheat field about a mile away from the bridge, as Justin instructed.

"Wait for me here, Lieutenant," Justin said. "This shouldn't take more than an hour. Two at the most." His watch read seventeen minutes to eleven. "If I'm not back by one o'clock, you take off without me and head back for Chicago."

The lieutenant smiled, nodded, and pulled the chopper door shut as Justin leaped lightly to the ground. He was wearing the commando suit again, but his only weapon this time was the .38. He also carried a black-painted contraption strapped to his chest in the exact center of an X-shaped harness that crossed over his front and back.

As he moved across the field toward the bridge, he wished that the moon were not so bright, but nothing could be done about that. He ran steadily for about half an hour, the expansion bridge looming up closer and closer in front of him; he enjoyed the feeling of giving his cramped muscles some exercise after the chopper ride.

Suddenly, he heard the yelping of dogs—those were close; apparently the dogs of Carlton—and then the faraway baying of hounds. At almost the same time, he spotted Andrea McKay bounding naked across the field behind him like a graceful gazelle.

God, but she is beautiful! Justin thought, with a twinge of regret that grew into a lump in his throat. Except for her madness, and for the fact that she was with SADIF, he could very easily have loved her. Even now, remembering the scene with her on top of the levee, he felt his loins growing warm.

But there was no time to think of that right now. He hid in a clump of bushes by the side of the road and grabbed her as she came by. He grabbed her, and she fought him like the mad creature she was until he hauled off and cold-cocked her on the point of her chin. She collapsed into his arms like a sack of potatoes.

She was surprisingly light as he made his way toward the bridge, where four soldiers and a captain were posted. There was no river traffic: in a top-secret alert, shipping had been warned away from the area for the twenty-four hours beginning at noon today. Also, both bridges into Carlton had been guarded by army troops since the same hour, permitting only those with bona-fide credentials to leave the island; no one was allowed to enter except for Carlton residents.

Passing the stolid soldiers, who'd been alerted for this drama by the command post and had been handpicked by the Old Man himself, Justin felt somewhat ridiculous carrying the naked woman across the bridge. It reminded him of a scene out of a play put on by maniacs. He heard the river lapping underneath the bridge and the dismal screeching of gulls.

Then Andrea was conscious, struggling in his arms. He saw her neck stiffen, then turn from side to side as she oriented herself. Then she was staring up into his face.

"Justin! Thank God you found me!" she said. "They have told me what you intend to do . . . what you *must* do, since I've been elected president. But I am not mad, Justin. I beg you . . . look . . . look behind my left ear."

"What are you talking about?" he said. He had stopped trotting and was holding her with her back to the bridge.

She was swaying against him. "Just look behind my left ear. . . ."

There was still time. He dropped to one knee, and she fell unconscious into his arms. He cradled her gently across his knee as if she were a baby. Brushing her hair back, he saw a small metal device implanted behind her ear.

The sight of it hit him like a heavy fist in the belly.

There was hope after all! Whatever the device meant, Andrea couldn't be killed until after a proper evaluation.

He picked her up and ran like hell back across the bridge. "Inform the command post!" he yelled at the startled captain. "H-Hour is in thirty minutes. All posts to be evacuated by then!"

The captain kept his attention carefully away from the naked Andrea. "Yessir!" He even clicked his shiny boots like a Nazi.

Ten minutes later, Justin was in the helicopter airbound with Andrea McKay. She was incoherent and lucid by turn—but Justin thought now that he had a valid clue as to why she went around in circles like that. The small contraption behind her ear definitely needed exploring. He had wrapped a blanket around her and bent over her where she was strapped on the bunk as the helicopter bounced away.

There was only one question he wanted to ask, and he yelled it at her over the rotors' noise: "Who did this to you, Andrea?"

Her answer was faint, but still distinguishable as he knelt over her. "Dr. Carew . . . Thelma Carew . . . and others. But Dr. Carew was chief of the operating team." Then she closed her eyes and seemed to be sleeping.

He tucked the covers around her, then went forward with the pilot. Below, he could see the people who had pursued Andrea on the moon-swept plain.

The sight filled him with disgust now. It was like one of the worst scenes out of *Uncle Tom's Cabin*, the hounds after a runaway slave.

But in this case, they were wrong. The "slave" had been subject to a small electronics master and had been running away from terror and into the safety of Justin Perry's arms. Also no one had really made a serious evaluation of whether Andrea was mad or not.

All the evidence had been based on Thelma's assessment of the situation. And Thelma had implanted the control behind Andrea's ear, apparently some kind of device that altered certain functions of the brain, controlled others.

Still, his heart was warmed; Andrea had remembered, and she had come to him.

"Are we clear, Lieutenant?"

"We're clear, sir."

The pursuers were still a hundred yards or so away from the bridge. Some of them might get hurt, maybe a few of them killed. But Justin didn't give a shit now. His only desire was to wipe Carlton out and then to get Andrea away somewhere to have that thing behind her ear looked at.

The helicopter banked eastward as he pressed the button in the crossed harness on his chest. At the same time, the helicopter leveled off. Below Justin, to the moonlit west, he would see the dike, the buildings, and the thoroughfares of Carlton. He'd lived there for nearly nine months, and had hated every minute of it. Except for the time he'd spent with Andrea McKay, in that sweet madness with her on the levee.

And it was exactly the levee that went first. He saw the flash of explosions at both ends and in the middle, like puffballs of red in a pinball game. And then the middle gave, curving in upon itself, as both extremities gave way backward, crumbling in a kind of graceful slow motion. The Mississippi leaped up suddenly like wild beasts, white tongues licking, and began to cover the island. It was a beautiful and horrible sight at the same time.

Then, the other charges went off. Monitering them, Justin saw that they were at the precise points of the compass, barring the north, which had given way to the water. He could hear a loud, thundering roar, louder than even the helicopter's blades, like a deep, tremendous belch in the earth's interior. Looking at his watch, Justin saw that it was 1:45 A.M. Practically all of the people in Carlton were probably in bed; it was a good clean way for them to die, he thought.

As for the pursuing party as the helicopter swept over their heads, Justin saw that they had drawn up short at the first explosions. They were on higher ground in the plain on this side of the river, and there was little chance that the Mississippi would rise that high. Reporters among them had a fantastic front-row seat for a sensational page-one story: PRESIDENT-ELECT BELIEVED DEAD IN MYSTERIOUS HOMETOWN EXPLOSION. The Russians would be appropriately discreet; they had always played the know-nothing, good-guy role in this operation anyway. And SADIF would gnash its teeth and creep away to plan more dirt.

But Andrea McKay had not died at all. She had been examined by CIA scientists, who found that the metal device indeed altered her brainwaves, making her appear mad or sane in turn. Thelma and Dr. Porter's injections, rather than calming her, had functioned as a catalyst to the apparatus, a kind of fuel and conductor at the same time.

"What do we do about Thelma?" Justin asked the Old Man once she'd been checked again. And had been found out to be very dirty goods indeed: *Dr. Thelma Carew Gavrilov; naturalized Soviet citizen; presiding member of Soviet Academy of Psychiatric Sciences; SADIF agent; expert in altering states of human consciousness using biotechnical and biochemical procedures; instrumental in experiments on antigovernment and Jewish dissidents in Soviet Union; staff psychiatrist at notorious Leningrad Psychiatric Hospital Number 9.*

Right now, Thelma Carew was under discreet house arrest on a farm outside of Washington, with her two children that Dante had brought over from London.

179

"She's a big fish that slipped through the net," the Old Man said grimly. "Now she's got to pay."

"What about her children?" Justin said.

The Old Man shrugged. "They'll just have to grow up orphans," he said. "What kind of a mother is that for decent kids to have any way? Besides, we coaxed a confession from her. She's the one that killed your aunt. She put on a black wig, made up her face, and poisoned the poor woman.

"Also, I know she told you a lot of guff about that girl in the truck that got blown up on the highway. She told you the girl was Betty—the *real* Andrea McKay—from your long-ago summer. Well, she was just fucking with your head, trying to get you started on a guilt trip, I suppose.

"But the girl blown up was just who we said she was—Carla Strickland, with orders to blow your ass up. Nobody knows what happened to that kid you screwed down in Orlando. She's probably married by now and settled down, with kids of her own. So . . . what do you want to do about the very slippery Dr. Carew?"

Justin's jaw tightened. "Make her kids orphans," he said. But he was glad that the girl on the highway hadn't been the Betty from his childhood.

By morning, Thelma Carew had disappeared without a trace, as had the island of Carlton and the president-elect of the United States.

Now, in Jamaica, Justin Perry waited for Andrea McKay to be released from the Marymount Sanatarium, where she'd been undergoing treatment for the past three months. And as he waited, he found himself thinking about God, and about his son, and about love, not necessarily in that order. God and love seemed to be a kind of confusing labyrinth, a maze as intricate and sometimes as tricky and misleading as the Old Man's assignment sheets.

None of what had happened to Andrea McKay, once she'd been marked for execution by the Old Man, was orthodox, or even permitted. Certainly none of it was in the assignment sheets that Justin had memorized that day at Riverview, and then had had to depart from like an editor penciling in new action and new ideas when the proposed ones refused to fit.

The same was true of the five photos that the Old Man had given him of probable SADIF agents to be on the lookout for: the unfortunate girl with the truckload of pumpkins on the highway, Mrs. Peters, Andrea McKay, Thelma Carew, and Fran Whittaker. All of them had turned out to be SADIF agents in the end, although Andrea's part had been cleverly coerced.

So there was something to be said about the Old Man's assignment sheets after, his careful plotting out of an adventure in which his agents functioned as actors, following a script until it could no longer be depended upon.

Still, there were times, such as with Andrea McKay, when the agent had to make decisions that sometimes went against the spirit and the letter of the sheets. How long had Justin known that he was going to save Andrea McKay, regardless of what the Old Man said? And then Andrea had come to him, in trust and love, and had given him the way.

Love. It was a strange word in his vocabulary, almost unknown in his sensations. He was a killer; brutal sometimes, gentle at other times. But never loving a woman, not since his wife's death. And loving his son as a father does. Until he had found Andrea McKay there on the levee, and something of her spirit had mingled with his. Thank God he hadn't killed her, he thought. It was about as close as he could get to God in these days.

As for Dr. Porter and the other SADIF agents at Riverview, they had been flushed out and done away with. Justin could have had Andrea treated there by the new professionals, but he had preferred to take her away to new and uncomplicated surroundings, like here in Jamaica.

The CIA had picked up the bill for the treatments, although Justin could easily have afforded it with the millions left to him by his real mother. But the Old Man had insisted, perhaps as a kind of atonement for having sent Justin to kill the wrong madwoman.

As for the American political system, it had recovered nicely from the onslaught of Andrea McKay; special elections had been held, in the absence of a vice-president from Andrea's party to take over after she disappeared. The incumbent Republican president had won hands down after he'd withdrawn the troops from Nicaragua and let it be known that perhaps he might have been shooting from the hip after all. Now the world was at peace again for a few more days, until SADIF should come back with another scheme to upset the tranquillity of things.

"Justin?"

He turned. She was standing near him, in a white dress and white shoes. A black nurse was with her. And Andrea was smiling. "They tell me that I can go home now."

He went to her and took her in his arms. She was the most beautiful, the most desirable woman he'd ever known. "I'm afraid home for you will be South America for the next few years," he said. The CIA had arranged for a ranch in Argentina, with the Argentinian government providing protection.

"Will you come and see me there?" she asked. Her large green eyes were warm, trusting. And inviting.

He felt his body heat all over. "I'll come to see you," he said, taking her bag from the nurse. "Now, there's somebody outside waiting to meet you," he said, taking her elbow and propelling her toward the exit.

"Who is waiting?" Andrea said.

Justin wrapped his arm around her as they walked down a lane of flaming hibiscus trees casting cool shadows on the ground.

"I want you to meet my son," Justin said. "He flew down with me. His name is Roger." And they walked out of the shadows into the sunlight.

Watch for

STUD SERVICE

next in **THE ASSASSIN** series
from Pinnacle Books

coming in May!